PETER S. GREENBERG spent almost forty years as
a lawyer, briefly as a prosecutor in Philadelphia and
as a law professor in Cleveland, and for most of the time,
as a commercial litigator in Philadelphia.
He lives in Florida and Vermont.

POTOMAC PRINCESS
AN ELECTION TALE

PETER S. GREENBERG

GREENVILLE PUBLISHING
DESTIN, FLORIDA

POTOMAC PRINCESS: AN ELECTION TALE.
Copyright © 2020 by Peter S. Greenberg.
All rights reserved. Printed in the United States of America.
For information, address Greenville Publishing,
1040 Highway 98 East, #415, Destin, Florida 32541.

ISBN 978 1-7354680-0-6 (paperback)
ISBN 1-7354680-1-3 (e-book)

First published by Greenville Publishing
August 2020

The not too distant future. . . .

CHAPTER 1

"So Kaitlyn, you've decided?"

"We're going ahead."

"Denying the nomination to a sitting President is a tall order."

"He's vulnerable. And incompetent."

"And you?"

"I'll be doing a lot again. Just like with your run."

"I lost, remember."

"You came close enough. And they made you Chief Justice to get you out of the way."

"I suppose. And you're running again for your House seat?"

"Why not? If Democrats put up a horse of average intelligence she wins in Philadelphia, so why would my constituents bother that I'm busy with a presidential campaign. If they even know. It's not like they love our President Bromwell. And it's no different than when you ran. Except this time it's not my father.

"True. And your candidate, your Senator Burnett. How does he compare to the horse?"

"He's a good man."

"Is that enough? Being good in bed doesn't count, you know."

"That was uncalled for. Besides, the bar's not very high. Bromwell's dumb as a brick. The horse would be a step up. Wilson's a genius by comparison."

"Perhaps I should try again."

"Let it go. We tried, you lost. You're Chief Justice, you probably have more power than anyone but the president. And last year you had three quarters of your colon out."

"But. Yes. Look Kaitlyn, just think it over. You know how hard it's going to be."

"Nobody else calls me 'Kaitlyn'."

"Nobody else is your father."

"I'd like to think so."

Chapter 2

Roger Newley is making a brave effort to keep his erection long enough to finish. Meredith Simmons is lying silent and largely motionless underneath. He feels short on oxygen, he really needs to make time for the gym. He thinks of Kati Case. It's worked before. Imagines unbuttoning her lacy white blouse, pictures gently playing with the small firm boobs he's never seen. Hard pink nipples? He's getting there. Hears Kati moaning as he pulls down her panties. Black? A thong? Comes. Rolls off as Meredith sighs with relief.

"Well, that's over," she says. And I do mean over."

Roger doesn't bother to respond.

"You don't care?"

"About?"

"That we're through. Finis. Etc."

"We are? We just fucked."

"For the last time."

Roger Newley starts getting it. His thoughts immediately turn to Meredith's father, Brett Simmons, ranking member of the Senate Judiciary Committee, and wonders about how to replace a key source. "What's suddenly happened?"

"I'm seeing someone new."

"So who's the lucky guy?" he asks, hoping it's not another reporter who'll poach his inside stories.

Otherwise, he's not much disappointed if this is the last he's going to see of Meredith's cramped, hospital white, Capitol Hill studio, or the battleship gray Ikea sofa bed that gives him back spasms. He *is* going to miss the Senate-perk box seats for Nats games that she gets from her father. Meredith's a big fan with photos of the 2019 championship team filling up her limited wall space.

For Roger Newley, Meredith is OK. A little overweight, maybe 10 pounds, her nose is a bit pointy, her eyes are a little too close together, her chin is kind of weak, but she's not bad. Not so stimulating, she doesn't do much but move from one non-profit to another, and except for baseball, there isn't much to talk about. But women aren't really Roger Newley's game. He's straight, that's not the issue, it's just so hard to keep things going. You should settle down, give us grandchildren like your sister, get a job that pays something and move out of that dump -- he hears it but to no effect. Why's it necessary, after all, he gets laid as often as he needs to, things aren't so bad, and that's maybe enough.

"Do you really care?" she asks. "You were probably thinking of Kati Case while we were doing it. She's all you talk about."

This obviously hits close to home, but Roger maintains his composure. "She's a friend. She's an important person." And she's not in my league.

"Well guess what, I was thinking of her too. Too bad it didn't get me off."

Roger ponders this but says nothing.

"It's not a guy," Meredith adds, not sure if he's gotten the point.

Roger stays silent.

"It's Tess Brathwaite."

He knows Tess Brathwaite slightly, she's high up prosecuting frauds at the Justice Department, and he's dealt with her when he's been stuck covering legal stories. He has nothing to add.

So Meredith keeps talking, suddenly consoling. "I'm sure this must be terribly emasculating for you, I am sorry. I hope you can pick up the pieces and move on."

He's moved on enough other times. He just shrugs, pulls on his pants. "Good night and good luck" he adds, but she misses the journalistic reference.

Chapter 3

Kati Case arrives. So does Carter Howell's gin. The waiter looks at her inquiringly. She orders an iced tea.

Kati is wearing a thin white sweater with a short v-neck that shows nothing of her slight cleavage, and tight black dressy jeans that highlight her cute rear, which at 37 attracts as much attention as ever.

"You're ten minutes late. For you, early. On the wagon?" he asks.

"Busy afternoon," she answers.

"No doubt. At my age, you never know if you'll still be around at dinner. So get it while you can, I say."

"Oh stop. You've been drinking the same thing at lunch here, and everywhere else, for 60 years. Beefeater, two ice cubes, twist, no Vermouth. You don't even have to order."

This is true. He's well known at the Benjamin Rush. But it could be the Palm, or Charlie Palmer, or anywhere. Because he's Carter Howell, and seems to have been around since time began. Deputy Director at the CIA, undersecretary for multiple cabinet posts, White House advisor, in his spare time writing screenplays in Hollywood. Mostly under the radar but invariably proximate to power. Now returned from his last rodeo, the ambassadorship to the remnants of the British Empire, he's settled in as Special Adjunct Professor of Political History at Georgetown. And bestower of whenever-its-needed advice all over town. Especially to Kati Case.

"There are rumors," he says. I'm supposing you wish to discuss this undertaking I'm hearing about."

"Of course you've already heard."

"You're biting off quite a mouthful."

"So what's new?"

He smiles. She can be rather charming, this very pretty, skinny young thing, but tough enough too. "But this is close to unprecedented. The only elected president to not be renominated was Pierce in 1856. Caught up in the dispute over the Kansas-Nebraska Act. Not much relevance there. Tyler, Fillmore, Arthur, but none of them had actually been elected. Of course, Andrew Johnson. Obviously a special case."

The waiter slinks back. Carter Howell orders the open-faced sirloin sandwich, very rare, she a Cobb salad, vinaigrette. "Nothing else?" the waiter asks her. If I wanted something else, I'm guessing I'd have mentioned it, Kati thinks. But being a political and public person, she offers only no thanks.

Kati Case takes a certain perverse pleasure in being at the Benjamin Rush -- which serves almost exclusively meat to almost exclusively men. Benjamin Rush, she took it upon herself to find out, was a signer of the Declaration; taught at the University of Pennsylvania (her alma mater); and has been called the father of American psychiatry. All dark wood and dim lighting, with portraits of be-wigged founding fathers (one of whom she assumes is Rush himself, although she's never checked), the BR is perfect for clandestine meetings of cabinet members and lobbyists, Senators and contributors.

"Even Reagan couldn't block Ford from renomination," Carter Howell continues to expound. "And Ford was rather dull and hadn't even been elected. Ted Kennedy couldn't beat Jimmy Carter, who was wildly unpopular."

"Although there was that dead girl at the bottom of the salt pond," she points out. "What about LBJ?"

He smiles. "Of course, that's somewhat encouraging. But he had the sense to bow out. Bromwell won't."

Kati picks up on that. "He's far worse than LBJ. LBJ was smart. Politically skilled. Actually accomplished things. He was just done in by Vietnam. Bromwell's a fool and has the Iran fiasco."

"Indubitably. The economy stinks. And sending troops into Iran over a false rumor they were going to attack Israel, then pulling out when they came under attack because we were too incompetent to prevent the Revolutionary Guard from somehow discovering what was coming, that was truly appalling. Bay of Pigs times ten. And this was American military, not a bunch of crazy Cubans."

"Speaking of crazy Cubans, what do you hear about Villar."

Carter Howell laughs. "Nothing really. I'd expect that he'd want out of Miami. Biscayne Boulevard is under water half the time, and in South Beach they're kayaking from Meridian to Ocean Drive whenever it storms. Or there's a high tide. But running for President? Should I have heard something more?" He once heard everything. Closeted over at Georgetown, is he beginning to lose touch?

He excuses himself to go to the Men's, grumbling about his blood pressure meds. A pharmaceutical lobbyist who Kati thinks she once had a meeting with, heading to a table where an FDA chemist is waiting, leers at her as he slides by. Part of being Kati Case.

Princess of the Potomac, the Washington Herald society pages once called her, to her considerable disgust. Back when the Herald was still a real paper with society pages, the one Roger Newley thought he was signing on for.

Carter Howell's sirloin arrives swimming in blood. The waiter handles it like the Crown Jewels. Kati's salad lands in front of her, treated with the patent disdain girl food deserves. Or maybe she's imagining. "Good Lord, couldn't they . . . drain it or something," she says, cringing at his plate. "Is it dead?"

"Did you know my mother was French? She'd haunt me if I ordered it medium."

He cuts into his meat, Kati spears half a hard boiled egg. "So anyway -- "

"Back to business. Certainly there's a chance. Everything you say about Bromwell is right on. Although I wonder -- and I realize you have a rather . . . personal attachment -- but Senator Burnett? I'm fond of Wilson, you know. But is he up to it?"

Kati frowns. "Running? Or governing?"

"Running's no problem. Well-known Senator, handsome, I assume big money backing at home in California, no black marks to speak of. Except, perhaps, you, but nowadays who cares. As president, not so sure."

She hesitates for a moment. "He's good enough. With the right cabinet and all. And me."

"That, I scarcely would underestimate, Kati dear. So go for it, the worst you can do is lose. You'll be no less lovely for it."

"Are you hitting on me?" she laughs.

He sighs. If only. "At this point the only thing I can hit on is the floor if I try to get up without my cane. Oh, but to be 20 years younger, Kati Case. Maybe 40."

"And straight."

"But 40 years ago I was. Sometimes. By the way, how's your father?"

"OK. The oncologist thinks he's clean. Of course, he'd like to be the one to take down Bromwell, but I think I've convinced him that Chief Justice is enough. And you?"

He's old now, she knows, no longer merely "gracefully aging." The sprinkles of hair left on top are white, his eyeglasses are thick as the ends of binoculars, he's grown out a scruffy gray beard because, he says, he's tired of his shaking hands drawing blood when he shaves. The tweed herringbone suits he wears in any weather have seen better times. Far from the man-about who charmed sleek ladies and, in the shadows, pretty men. His wife of fifty-odd years was finally lost to Alzheimer's not long before his appointment in England. Freed from any need to masquerade, and no longer giving a damn, he returned from London with Desmond Fenwick and openly installed him in the Kalorama townhouse. Only to have poor Desmond drop dead right outside the Dupont Circle Metro station.

"Well enough. A bit lonely at times. So many have passed on now. But a few of us are still around, so I get by. You help."

They finish. He insists on taking the check. As always. She slowly walks him out into blinding March sunshine. Washington is already becoming uncomfortable, everyone talks about the warming but nothing gets done. She thinks he must be hot in his tweeds as she puts him in a cab.

Chapter 4

The black Mercedes SUV glides around Chevy Chase Circle into Maryland and continues along Connecticut Avenue. The driver is careful, keeps to the speed limit. In less than a mile, an unmarked car pulls out of leafy Bradley Lane and on go the blue lights on top of the dash. Malcolm Douglas looks in the rearview, sighs, and pulls over.

By the time the cop's walked up, he's holding license, registration, and, on top, House of Representatives ID, out the window. The cop looks awfully young, like a high school kid in a Halloween police outfit.   Pasty-faced to start, he turns a shade whiter as he sees whom he's stopped. Whiter shade of pale, Malcolm Douglas thinks, always wondered what that meant.

Officer Nesbitt tries to play defense. "Er, sir, um. I thought. Taillight. Looked." Pause. "Out?"

Malcolm laughs. "What you thought, son, is that a Black man drove by in a Mercedes, and you thought you were on to something."

"Oh, not at all, no sir. Everyone speeds down Connecticut once it's dark -- not you, of course -- and we need to be . . . on the lookout. Sir. For things."

"Now don't give me that Bull, young man. You're new on the job, I'm guessing." He doesn't sound really furious, Officer Nesbitt is relieved to hear. The voice, deep, low, carefully modulated, perfected in years of House debates.

"Yes, sir. And proud -- "

"Certainly. I'm 10 terms in the House, and pulling me over is like a rite of passage for you fellows. I used to get riled up. I'd call and complain, I'd get a song and dance from whoever they decided would be the one to calm me down. But I've learned, there's only so much you can change, and only so fast. So now all I'm going to say is, let it be a lesson to you. And particularly, keep it in mind if you ever think of using that gun they gave you."

"You're not angry, sir?"

"Of course I'm angry. Don't you think I should be? And what would you have done if I hadn't handed you that House ID? Hauled me down to the station for some investigation? Don't think because I'm not going to eat you alive, that I'm not angry."

"Yes sir, sorry sir."

"Let's let it go at that. Have a good night, son."

Almost home, CarPlay cuts off NPR and tells Malcolm he has a text. Siri-voice asks if she should read it. Yes. "I didn't get that," says Siri-voice. "I'll try again. You have a message. Should I read it?"

"Yes!" he shouts.

"Reading your Message. 'Hi Malcolm, it's Kati Case. Something important I want to discuss. Not urgent. Call when it's convenient. Have a good night.'"

Since her first term, he's sure Kati Case is a player. He's been around long enough to know. He wonders what she wants. Probably Ways and Means business. As he pulls into the driveway, Malcolm Douglas figures Glenda will be getting dinner on the table, and figures Kati Case can wait until tomorrow.

Chapter 5

EAR TO THE GROUND
By Roger Newley

The Ear hears explosive news. The Ear's well-placed sources are telling us that Senator Wilson Burnett (D. Cal.) is gearing up for a challenge to President Daniel Bromwell for the Democratic nomination! Although Bromwell looks vulnerable -- suffering an anemic 35% in the most recent TruNews approval polling averages -- if Burnett makes the race, it would be the first meaningful primary challenge to an incumbent president since Senator Edward ("Ted") Kennedy unsuccessfully tried to seize the nomination from President Jimmy Carter in 1980.

Our sources aren't saying at this point what backing Burnett expects if he pursues his audacious ploy. However, The Ear has picked up whispers that Representative Kati Case (D. Pa.) could be high up in the campaign. Case, the daughter of Supreme Court Chief Justice and former Pennsylvania Senator Paul Winthrop Case -- who lost his bid for the Democratic nomination four years ago -- is a member of the House's so-called progressive wing. The Ear wonders if this presages an anti-Bromwell coalition between the Democrats' left wing and the establishment center where Burnett has generally situated himself, and where Bromwell's base of support remains.

The Ear hears only silence on whether Case's estranged husband, Governor Sam Jensen (D. N.H.), is on board with a Burnett run. Case and Jensen have always maintained that they keep their marriage and their politics completely apart, even before their separation.

Roger Newley stops. Finger poised over the delete key, he considers whether Kati Case would be OK with the final paragraph. It's accurate and neutral, sort of relevant, and says nothing that isn't already well known. But still, it wasn't included in what she told him to write, and the last thing he needs is to get on Kati's bad side.

He exits his bedroom/workspace (which doesn't deserve to be called an office) and rummages in the fridge, coming up with a can of lemonade and a two-day old chicken taco. He pops the taco in the microwave sitting on the beige and gold-flecked laminate counter. He's still in his red and yellow plaid pajamas (clearance rack, Jockey Outlet at National Harbor). Working from home is encouraged now that his employer, the Washington Herald, is much reduced in stature and funding -- which is better than the alternative, total dissolution.

The crabbed newsroom space that the accounting boys allow is even less comfortable for Roger Newley than the corner of his bedroom, so he composes columns and stories whenever he can in his 1970's garden apartment halfway to Baltimore. Convenient for 95 though, for when he has to cover stuff in the District, or talk face-to face to sources. He can see the highway in the distance through the undernourished-looking trees, likely choking on the fumes.

Taco and drink in hand, he bypasses the very dark, formal and thoroughly out-of-place dining table and drops onto the almost as dark and unsuitable brown faux-Victorian loveseat. Wildly uncomfortable, the curving wood back is too low and hits him in the middle of the neck, the seat is worn-down and stony. But the furniture was free, gifted by his parents when they migrated from 73rd and Broadway to the not-so-far-from-the-beach condo in Fort Myers, where they chose to decorate with a more tropical look. It's for you, they told him, your sister (a very prominent cardiologist living in Westwood with her big-firm attorney husband and two very beautiful children) doesn't need it (and you do).

This wasn't the plan when Roger graduated with honors from the English Department at Colgate, picked up a journalism M.A from Columbia, and immediately got an apparently prestigious job at the Herald. Write, write, write his 11th grade English teacher at Collegiate told him a long time ago, and write he has. But writing, it turns out, is not so prestigious, and definitely not too lucrative, although it leaves him time to work on the novel that he fantasizes about but isn't getting anywhere with.

He turns on Sports Center. Above the TV is an unsigned print, possibly Don Quixote, perhaps Bolivar, by a Venezuelan abstract artist his parents met at a hotel in Curaçao.

Maybe he should check in with Kati. He'd like to drive down and discuss it at Starbucks, but he's sure she's too busy to even take a phone call.

He dumps the dishes in the sink and runs some water so the taco remnants won't congeal, returns to his computer, deletes the unapproved add-on paragraph, and flips through his notes looking for whatever other rumors he can fill out the column with. He chooses an aide to a Congresswoman from New Mexico going home to run for the legislature; and a Treasury analyst taking a hedge fund job in Connecticut.

Roger Newley sends The Ear off into cyber space, to a person Somewhere whose name he isn't sure of, who will barely read it, not notice that it has a rumor more important than the usual, and stick it on some back page with the op-Ed's and the editorials Then he takes a nap.

*   *   *

Good, Newley got the story right, Kati Case thinks. She likes him, he's reliable. Of course, he has a massive crush she takes constant advantage of. Girls learn these things. You feel guilty and you do it anyway, and when you need to, you do it some more. Guys do it too, but they're so single-minded, just getting into your pants, so they're more transparent. Roger Newley deserves a nice girlfriend.

She wonders, working on the start-up for the campaign, does it bother her that Wilson Burnett himself isn't more involved? He's a big picture guy, she knows that. Her father got involved too much, he thought he had to edit everything, it made her crazy. Now he can do whatever he wants with his Supreme Court opinions.

She's relieved Wilson Burnett likes her idea of putting Malcolm Douglas on the ticket from the start. He's been in the House forever, he's smart, conscientious, hard-working, savvy, and totally a straight arrow, and as Chairman of Ways and Means, he's been kind of a mentor for her. And he could pull in lots of Black voters. She wonders why he hasn't responded to her text.

Would my father have listened to me if I told him who to run with, she asks herself. Probably not. Would he have listened to Lenore? Probably. Whatever my mother said, ruled.

Chapter 6

Hello Kati-
Haven't forgotten you. Got your text but got laid up in Walter Reed
with my ulcer after Glenda put too many damn jalapeños in the chili.
Get back to you when they let me out

Malcolm

Chapter 7

Kati Case has particular distaste for Andrea Weatherill Jarrett's Capitol soirées, invitations to which are in the utmost demand and attendance at which is *de rigueur*. Of course she's invited. And, duty bound, she shows up.

Kati herself was forced to become a party hostess, and her life altered seismically, the February night in her senior year when, with light drizzle and temperatures around freezing, Lenore Case -- driving from a Women for Case buffet in tony Chestnut Hill to a fundraiser in Center City (in the same Philadelphia Congressional District Kati now represents) -- missed a turn on the misty, snaking Lincoln Drive, slid into a tree, and broke her neck.

Shortly after the funeral, Kati withdrew her M.B.A applications and took her mother's place behind the scenes for Paul Winthrop Case, Harvard magna cum laude, Yale Law Review, well-regarded Assistant U.S. Attorney -- but for all that, politically clumsy. For him to get the Democrats' nomination for D.A. (the equivalent of being elected in ultra-blue Philadelphia); move on to Congress; and finally, get elected to the Senate, Lenore pulled the levers and staged the events. That became Kati's job.

Not particularly close with her mother -- who possibly, Kati later considered, viewed her only-child daughter as a serious competitor -- Kati nonetheless paid very close attention to what Lenore was up to, and knew how to take over the reins when she was abruptly and unexpectedly gone.

Truth be told, she was happy to move on from college, where she was a reluctant Tri-Delt who stayed the sorority course at her mother's insistence ("you're networking") and was annoyingly pursued by frat boys who, with one sad exception, she had little interest in. Her virginity wasn't at issue, lost at 16. Why say lost, she thought, when she knew exactly where it always had been, and precisely where she left it -- in the backseat of the car of a boy from North Jersey she had met two nights before, parked on a dimly lit and peaceful beach block in Harvey Cedars. The experience was painful, but not uninteresting, and blessedly short thanks to his singular lack of control. It has potential, she concluded.

She was somewhat puzzled why boys were so interested. Flat-chested, skinny and narrow-hipped, kind of built like them she thought, except of course for her point-of-entry which they were so anxious to get at. What a pretty girl, she was constantly told: light brown hair framing high cheekbones, very round and deep brown eyes, tiny turned-up nose, perfect inviting lips.

In her freshman year, a college friend of her father's, a long out-of-the-closet Manhattan art dealer, suggested she model, at least part time. "Just start doing your face a little and grow your hair out of that pixie thing, and you're runway ready. Or you could just go up and do photo layouts. I know some great fashion guys. Candice Bergen did it back in the day, you know, just took the train up from Philly. And she was dating some actor, too."

"George Hamilton," Kati replied, having heard about it at orientation. "She also flunked out."

At 37, still no lines on her face, just a few pounds heavier, Kati Case grudgingly walks into Andrea Weatherill Jarrett's 5100 square foot Fairfax County Georgian, where Andrea has chosen to stage the event rather than at her somewhat less ample 6-bedroom Georgetown townhouse. It's mobbed, she seems to have invited the world. Worse yet, made clear in bold letters on the invites, it's a HISTORY THEME MASQUERADE.

Nonetheless, Kati comes as a cat, recycling an outfit from three Halloweens ago, black sweater, tiny black skirt over black tights, headband with little pointy black ears, mascara cat nose and whiskers. She looks adorable, to the annoyance of the hostess.

Andrea Weatherill Jarrett is in a long, puffy, blue and white dress with a white apron front, cut low enough to show a fair amount of her pale and sizable boobs. Her long blonde hair is stuffed into a matching white cap-thing that looks to Kati like a linen lampshade. Holding a small American flag and a knitting needle, which makes no sense Kati thinks, apparently she's Betsy Ross.

"Kati, dear," Andrea greets her, waving a Bloody Mary, "you're just darlin'. But you need to be historical, girl."

"I'm one of Thomas Jefferson's cats," Kati replies. "There was quite the problem with rats in the barn at Monticello, loads of them." She bares her teeth. She has no idea whether Jefferson had rats, cats or a giraffe at Monticello.

Kati views Andrea Jarrett, who isn't that much older, as from a different generation. Maybe a different planet. Is it all from the childbearing experience Kati lacks and intends to continue to miss out on? Not interested in further pursuing Jefferson's vermin, Andrea takes a hit of Bloody Mary and changes the subject. "I've been hearin' rumors that our little Kati's gettin' ready for some big movin' and shakin'."

Kati notices that the hostess's Kentucky twang seems awfully strong, figures she's already halfway loaded, and just shrugs. "I haven't seen Samuel yet," Andrea adds.

Of course, Andrea Weatherill Jarrett knows full well what the story is with Kati and Sam Jensen, who nobody calls "Samuel" and who rarely appears in the Capital. Kati looks up at the enormous chandelier they're standing under, focuses on its twinkling glass chips that seem to be giving off oddly blue light, and composes herself. "He has a state to run," is all she says.

Teddy Roosevelt walks by -- burly guy, pith helmet, khaki jacket and pants, wire-rimmed glasses, bushy paste-on mustache -- and gives Kati a pat on the ass. Andrea thinks to herself that Kati gets too much attention. "You don't know the half of it girl," Teddy says over his shoulder

"Who the fuck is that?" Kati asks.

"Some General? Friend of Beaufort, Brandon golfs with him, I think. Retired not long before the Iran mess, if he's the guy. Turley , or Hurley, or somethin'."

"Wonder what I don't know half of?"

"Men like to grab your ass?" She laughs. "But you most surely do know that, darlin'. How's Senator Burnett?"

"In California." She turns away, heads for the bar. Bitch, she thinks. "Slut," Andrea Weatherill Jarrett mutters to herself, but three Bloody Mary's along, loud enough for Kati to hear. Bitch, Kati thinks.

She gets a very light Gin and Tonic, hoping to escape and drive home soon, and goes to mingle in what might be an enormous formal dining room with another twinkling chandelier, and with wallpaper that looks an awful lot like a plantation scene -- although the slaves seem to have been edited out. Alert in case Teddy Roosevelt comes by again, she listens to Priscilla Dunlap, dressed as herself and who's on the Board, go on about an upcoming Smithsonian Exhibit of Reconstruction Tablecloths; runs into her father wearing his Chief Justice robes ("John Marshall") and reprimands him for coming without a date; and nods her head in agreement as Arizona Republican Congressman Mario Santana -- daringly, Fidel Castro -- complains about how the food has deteriorated in the Members Dining Room. Kati sees Meredith Simmons, apparently a pirate but maybe a somewhat plump Johnny Depp, heading over and starts to move away. Roger Newley's girlfriend, she recalls, although heaven knows why. But Roger is nowhere in sight, and Meredith is apparently accompanied by a lithe and angular Black woman, vaguely familiar, maybe from Justice, in a long dark dress slit up the side and impressive dreads with a rainbow of beads. Is it a costume?

Brandon Jarrett, dressed in crimson bell-bottoms and a purple tie-dyed shirt open to almost his navel, and wearing a shoulder-length wig, intercepts her before she can sneak out. "Not leavin' sweet thing?" he asks.

"Get rid of the drawl. Who are you?"

"Sixties Hippie. You?"

"Felix the Cat. Historical cartoon celebrity."

That gets a blank look. Up from humble beginnings, son of a plumber from Trenton, Brandon Jarrett made it through Rutgers with loans and did well enough to get into North Carolina Law School. Without stellar grades or professors' recommendations to lucrative law firms, he was scraping along on slip-and-falls and DUI's as a solo practitioner in Charlotte when a trip to the Kentucky Derby made his fortune. Invited by a law school pal to a party way above his station, he charmed and bedded Andrea Weatherill, the surprisingly horny heiress to old Kentucky slave, tobacco, bourbon, and horse money, and managed to knock her up. After old Beaufort Weatherill calmed down, he decided it was just as well to have flighty Andrea off his hands; and that it could be worse than a fellow who at least has a respectable law degree and who Beaufort could make something of. So after Brandon expeditiously changed his registration to Republican, and learned the proper way to talk, Beaufort financed his way to a seat in the legislature, and before long to Congress.

"Stick around," he says to Kati. "I don't like this horseshit any more than you do, and I need someone to talk to who won't give me seizures from boredom. Or we can discuss Ways and Means."

Brandon Jarrett's been making clear for some time that he'd like nothing better than to get his hands on Kati. So far he's failed, although truth be told, he isn't entirely unappealing. Dark and square-jawed, kind of handsome in a bland sort of way, the Weatherill's haven't completely destroyed all of his up-from-the streets charm. And his deep blue eyes tend to get her attention. She knows he's managed to bed quite a number of Capitol desirables. Then again, so has she.

"Why don't I show you the upstairs," he offers. "This place has 11 bedrooms. Damned if I know why we need them. One of the girls is off to college, the other's leaving next year. Eleven fucking bedrooms."

The bitch called me slut, it would really serve her right, Kati starts rationalizing. And he's attractive enough, he's been trying for so long. What the Hell, she thinks, I could stand to get laid.

He goes up first, she rendezvous at a room at the end of a long corridor lined with prints of happy antebellum scenes. An empty room except for a queen-sized bed frame and mattress that Brandon Jarrett has hastily covered with a clean teal sheet. The walls are bare, except for dirty gray wallpaper peeling at the corners.

"Wow, so atmospheric," Kati laughs as Brandon turns the lock. "Don't need all these bedrooms, huh?"

"Makin' do with what we've got," he says, slipping back into Kentucky speak. "Still redecoratin'."

It goes rather well. She comes on fast, kissing him, playing her tongue around as he pulls her very tight. "You might want to take your ears off," he says, catching his breath.

"Just the ears?"

"Whatever. Remember, no noise."

"I'm a soundless fuck, lucky for you."

He fondles her small and firm left breast, licks her very erect right nipple. "They big enough?" Kati laughs, grabbing between his legs.

"Big enough?" he responds, totally hard.

"It'll do. Nice girth." She gets him in her mouth.

Then it's his turn, he works his way down her, rolling his tongue on her best place. Keeping her word, she doesn't make a sound despite a particularly compelling orgasm. She gets on top, he gets inside her, she rolls her hips as he pushes up, and to her surprise, she comes again as he fires off.

They briefly lie silent, his arm around her. "You should give more parties," Kati says. "And we'd better get back downstairs."

Hoping she hasn't been missed, Kati Case hastily fixes up her smudged cat nose and whiskers, adjusts her pointy ears, and goes down to say her goodbyes, giving especially warm thanks to Andrea Weatherill Jarrett for a lovely evening.

Chapter 8

Malcolm Douglas walks up behind Glenda as she stands over the stove. "Evening, darling." What's cooking." He's tall, a good 6'4", and quite a bit wider than in his playing days, and when he goes to the gym, he's still tough in the paint.

Seemingly half his size, she looks up at him. "Just plain roast chicken with some thin gravy a baby could handle. Keeping you safe on the tasteless diet."

"Yeah. Stay away from the damn peppers. There's something we need to talk about."

"Not while I'm trying to cook. Go sit down and have your Jack. Just a little, and put some water in like the doctor said."

Grumbling about ruining good sour mash, he heads for the living room, drops down into the old black leather recliner he's been sitting in for fifteen-odd years, and turns on the Wizards game before Glenda calls him in to dinner.

"Kati Case came by my office today," he tells her when they sit down.

"She's on the Ways and Means? And?"

"Wilson Burnett's going to try to take the nomination from the schmuck in the White House."

"I read some rumor -- "

"More than a rumor. It's happening. She's going to be high up in the campaign."

"Aren't the two of them?" She frowns. Glenda and Malcolm Douglas have been together for 40-odd years and neither has considered, for a minute, straying.

"It's what I hear," he answers, "but not for us to judge. In any event." He pauses. Takes a deep breath. Puts down his fork.

"Stomach again?"

"I'm fine. What she wanted to see me about was, they want me to run with him. For Vice. And they want to announce it up front."

"Malcolm! What did you -- "

He reaches across the table and takes her hand. "That we would need to talk. You and me."

"Then start talking. What exactly did she say ?"

"That they needed someone solid. Experienced. Honest. Capable. With presence. And with very dark skin, I told her, and she laughed and said that'd help too. The girl doesn't bullshit."

"How are you with that?"

He shrugs. "You know, when you've been around as long as I have, you learn about reality. As a rule, White folks are going to want to vote for White folks, Black folks want to vote for Black folks. It's the way of the world, and if it's changing slowly, it isn't fast enough, but I can't make it quicker. So you play the game with the rules that happen to be out there, and if you're lucky, you use it to make things better."

She sighs. "I suppose. But Malcolm, do you want it?"

He takes off his black bifocals and wipes them with a blue napkin. "Here's what I said. I was perfectly happy teaching history and coaching basketball in Cleveland Heights. Then folks put me up for Council, and I won, and that was OK because it was just some more work to do, but I kept teaching and coaching. And then they ran me for the House, and I won, and I just kept winning, and here we are all these years." He waves his hand, indicating the nondescript four-bedroom rancher that they bought when prices were more manageable, and stayed in, raising a boy and a girl, and mostly paying it off. "But to tell the truth, I'm never as happy as when I'm back in the Heights, in our little old house on Edgehill we started out with, with Lenny Pawalcz and his family on one side and Jin Park and his on the other, going down to dinner on Coventry and having folks come up to shake hands. Taking the train with Lenny down to the Browns games, bad as they were. Going -- "

"Enough Malcolm. I was there. Do. You. Want. It?"

"Being President is the furthest thing from what I want."

"Vice President?"

"Same."

Glenda shakes her head. "No it's not. President, I understand. With your ulcers and all. But Malcolm. It's such an honor."

"Yes."

"And the country needs to get rid of that Bromwell. You didn't say, what do you think of Senator Burnett?"

"Fine. Honest man. Not as sharp as Kati, but he'd do."

She stands up, walks behind his chair, and puts her arms around him. "You know I love you and I always will, no matter what. And I know who you are Malcolm Douglas. You don't want to do it. And you know you can't say no."

He gets up too. They're both sniffling, and he wipes a tear off her face. "Glenda Peoples Douglas, you do know me too well."

Chapter 9

They keep telling us to reach across the aisle, Kati Case thinks, so consider it a very worthwhile exercise in bipartisanship. A Republican, it turns out, who knows where all the right parts are, and how to use them.

I suppose I brought it on myself, she concedes, wearing that cat outfit with the tiny skirt that barely covers my ass and shows off my legs -- my best part they say, and they distract guys from how little my boobs are.

Is Kati feeling guilty? Kind of. But it's not like she goes hopping from bed to bed. It's sort of monogamous with Wilson. Although he still goes home to his wife. Why am I thinking I'm guilty anyway, she asks herself? Bet Jarrett isn't.

What would Lenore say? Better, why ask? She'd go to Confession, offer some holy repentance. Not that she'd ever have done it to begin with.

Chapter 10

6 A.M. The President of the United States, tossing in bed since 4, stumbles into the Oval Office. The First Lady remains snoozing. The President is trailed by Lanny Feldbaum, whom he's known since high school back in Niles, where Lanny managed his election as Student Council President; and Artie, 35 pounds of shaggy brown six-month old dog of nondescript origins (like me, the President has purportedly said) who the President and First Lady dote on now that the children are grown and gone.

Lanny Feldbaum's first task of the day as Presidential Accessory, a heretofore unknown and largely unofficial title, is to walk Artie. Leash in hand, he tries to secure the pup, especially hyper after a night in his cage. But Artie is too quick and races over to lift his leg on the Resolute Desk. Unfazed, Lanny Feldbaum grabs the Presidential Phone and dials up the cleaning crew.

On top of the Resolute desk is a large pile of memos, reports, analyses, studies, and miscellaneous paperwork that's slowly been accumulating. "Get someone to go through this crap and tell me if anything's important," the President of the United States tells Lanny Feldbaum, whose job is to delegate this task to one of the countless underlings whose purpose often puzzles the President.

Washington legend has it that the morning after his inauguration, President Bromwell, somewhat hung-over, walked into the Oval Office, saw a similar stack of paper on his desk, and exclaimed "What am I fucking doing here."

Lanny Feldbaum has been along for the ride that's landed him, and the President, in the Oval Office. Working his way up the political ladder from Student Council, the President eventually arrived at the Illinois governor's mansion. There, he distinguished himself only by managing to not be indicted through a term and a half, a singular accomplishment that evaded an uncomfortable number of his predecessors. Four years ago, on a particularly airless Baltimore summer evening, minding his own business eating a large number of Blue Claws and downing a pitcher of beer at a Fells Point crab house, he was surprised by Walt Morelli, the head of the Democratic National Committee, who pulled up a chair and told him -- being that he's apparently honest, or at least hasn't been caught out, and isn't disliked by anyone -- he's been anointed compromise nominee as the solution to an irretrievably deadlocked convention.

Paul Winthrop Case, second in delegates, is offered the next Supreme Court seat -- indeed Chief Justice were it first to open up -- if he gracefully bows out. Kati Case analyzes the numbers, takes the temperature of various delegations, and talks him into taking the deal. In November, Daniel Bromwell, the compromise nominee renowned for nothing in particular, is narrowly elected President of the United States.

Having been a sound sleeper until his time in the Nation's Capital, the President of the United States now stares into space for much of the night, plagued by thoughts of floods and droughts, hurricanes and tornadoes, real estate collapses, terrorist attacks, viral outbreaks, general national malaise, "the Iran Fiasco," and matters of personal conscience.

His insomnia is bad enough that a psychologist, an expert in sleep deprivation, gets smuggled into the White House away from the annoying press corps for consultations. Don't use your computer after five o'clock, go to bed and wake up at precisely the same time every day, and if you awaken during the night, after 15 minutes get up and play solitaire with a deck of cards (not your phone or tablet), he instructs the President of the United States. "Total asshole," the President tells Lanny Feldbaum.

He often wonders why he's putting himself in for four more years of this. Now that his financial situation is more secure, he could just opt out. But he knows they won't let him.

A small bowl of plain, non-fat yogurt with blueberries on top and a cup of black coffee sit next to the Presidential Paperwork on the Resolute Desk, a sparse breakfast resulting from the admonition of the White House Physician that he should lose some weight. The President of the United States eats it without enthusiasm, washes it down with the coffee that provides enough of a caffeine hit to get him moving, and tells Lanny Feldbaum that he's off to swim a few laps in the White House Pool.

Chapter 11

Dear EAR

You are writre and tool. Fool. You say much, but falsehoods. Ce que je dis est vrai.

Listen to me. Je suis l'ange sombre de la vengeance. The time has come that I act. Then everyone will know who I am. Et elle saura ma valeur. Once upon a time a man came to the power. The power didn't care. Le pouvoir apprendra. This has happened in history and will again. Elle m'aimera.

Jesus Leroi.

*　　*　　*

The letter is addressed to THE EAR AT THE HERALD. No address but it gets there. It's written with smudged black pencil on a sheet of three ring paper. Roger Newley gets correspondence like this all the time. He goes on google translate. "What I say is true." (No doubt.) "I am the dark angel of vengeance." (I'll bet.) "She will know my worth."
(Lucky girl.) "The power will learn." (What?) "She will love me." (Luckier still.)

He calls the cops. They pick it up, see that it's gone through the mail, and call the FBI. The FBI checks it for prints, finds only Roger Newley's, doesn't bother to translate, doesn't see a threat, and it gets tossed in the "Investigate Later?" file.

Chapter 12

"Fuckin' A," Brandon Jarrett yells as his three-footer rims and stays out on the 18th. "Yours again. What's the damage?"

"Owe me $80," Evan Hurley, two-star general, U.S. Army (retired) answers. "Drinks on me."

After countless lessons paid for by Beaufort Weatherill, he's managed to get his game into the 90's, where it's comfortably plateaued. Beaufort's instruction: "You need to golf, boy. Just be respectable so you can play at Congressional and not embarrass yourself. Or me."

"I'm not athletic," he protested.

"It has nothin' to do with athletics. It's golf. Half of it's in your head. Just focus on gettin' it into the hole, just like you focus on puttin' your thing in whatever hole you feel like. The way you did when you knocked up Andrea."

He never quite got the analogy. Today, to the contrary, on a late March afternoon with Spring coming on, he loses several holes when his "focus" strays to a very sweet time with Kati Case.

Evan Hurley takes a big slug of his double Johnny Walker Black on the rocks, Brandon Jarrett sips Coors Lite. Six foot and 210 pounds, the same weight he's always carried, General Hurley is wearing a brown polo shirt, khaki slacks, and a black baseball hat with "West Point" in gold letters over his graying brush cut. Brandon Jarrett, by considerable contrast, is in a lime green shirt, white pants, black and white golf shoes, and a white visor that won't mess up his carefully gelled hair. "Election's about to get going," Hurley offers.

This states the obvious. Now that Congress finally passed The Expeditious Presidential Election Act (upheld by the Supreme Court on a 5-4 vote) and remedied the interminable rallies, debates, and money begging, campaigning for the nominations is limited to April through the national primary on the first Tuesday in July, with the two conventions at the end of the month. Brandon Jarrett just nods.

"Everyone is saying that fellow from California's going to make a run at Bromwell. Looks to me like the same-old, same-old the Democrats put up." He drinks some more. "Pull out the troops, raise the taxes, take away the cars, confiscate the guns, more rights for queers, give money away to those that won't earn it themselves."

Which maybe wouldn't be so bad, Brandon Jarrett muses. Somewhere inside, the Trenton Democrat, son of a union plumber, still lurks. But he knows to keep his head down, vote the right way, and not cause trouble. "Suppose so," he responds, figuring that whatever he says will get back to Beaufort.

"Better than that Bromwell, I guess. Who are the Republicans going to run?"

Brandon knows that a group of the usual old white men is gearing up, but discreetly professes ignorance. "Who'd you rather run against?" Hurley asks. "Bromwell or the California guy?"

He drinks down half his beer. "Well Bromwell's approval is in the toilet, like at 35%, but he is the incumbent and he has lots of cash. The RNC must have some polling numbers, but they're keeping them to themselves." Or at least they haven't shown them to Brandon Jarrett, who finds it largely irrelevant who the president is, as long as nobody does anything to screw up his safe Congressional District. And he's been thinking that a side benefit of a Burnett victory might be that he'll finally bring his wife to Washington, and Kati Case might have more free time.

General Hurley drains his Johnny Walker. "Things about Bromwell, you can't imagine. Maybe I should. . . . But. . . ." He stops there.

Brandon Jarrett looks puzzled but lets it drop.

Chapter 13

An accident on the Theodore Roosevelt Bridge has traffic into Arlington stopped dead. Kati Case allows her mind to wander, and it finds its way to Brandon Jarrett. He's been smiling at her on the House floor whenever she's in view, but they haven't spoken since the party. It's not tenable she knows -- taking turns screwing two men, both married. She is too, although in name only, so that's not so much a problem.

She's been married to Sam Jensen, boy wonder governor of New Hampshire, for four years. Smart and witty, nice looking and fair-haired, she met him aboard a DNC fund-raising cruise on the murky Potomac. Two drinks along, the twinkling red, white and blue lights strung over the deck began to look romantic; three drinks and she had her arm around his waist; one more and he kissed her. Things moved along from there. Never very motivated toward marriage, she thought maybe this guy was worth a try.

One year in, he confessed: he's bisexual, always has been, and he leans to men. It's not fair to her. They should lead separate lives. Etc.

Kati had sensed for a while that something was amiss, and the whole marriage thing had pretty much lost its charm anyway. Divorce would be fine.

But no, he said, it would be detrimental to his career. "That makes no sense," she argued.

He was adamant. Unless she needed a divorce to marry someone else, he refused to agree, and he was sure she wouldn't destroy him, and maybe herself, by going public.

"In this day and age, who cares? After Trump? In New Hampshire?" she pointed out.

"There's a lot of old New Englanders with old New England values. Every election breaks close, and I can't afford to lose votes."

"Give me a break. It's Boston suburbs and hippies. You could be sleeping with a goat and it wouldn't bother anyone."

"That's Vermont."

It's not worth arguing. He's in Concord most of the time anyway, and she discretely does whatever she wants.

The back-up inches over the bridge. Wilson Burnett has red-eyed into Reagan National that morning, met with staff, made an appearance on the Floor, and now waits in Kati Case's apartment.

He's dozing on the couch, TV on to the Lauren Baxter Hour on TruNews, when she walks in. She plops down next to him and kisses him on the cheek. Semi-stupefied, he gives her a little hug.

"Exhausted?" she asks.

"I'll say."

"Better get used to it. What's she have to say?"

He shrugs. "She was just introducing the guests when I fell asleep."

Kati goes to the kitchen, takes the gin out of the fridge where Carter Howell insists it must be kept, mixes in the tonic, not too much, and curses because there aren't any limes. TruNews drones on in the distance.

TruNews promotes itself as "Impartial and Interesting" and owns a big share of the profitable younger demographic, to the extent they bother with news on television. Lauren Baxter was born in San Clemente (growing up in close proximity to Nixon's Western White House), graduated from U.C.L.A (President of the Young Republicans), and headed across the country to work in the polling unit of the R.N.C. Blue-eyed and blonde, she was recruited for television and progressed: commentator at Fox; early morning anchor at MSNBC; and now, early evening star at TruNews.

Kati hands Wilson Burnett his drink and sits down on the crimson leather couch that she picked up with a matching recliner at a Raymor & Flanagan President's Day sale. Lauren Baxter is pointing out that the President's approval ratings are at a historical low and his campaign cash at a record high.

"So what?" Kati says. "Lauren is such a snake," she gratuitously adds.

"Really, Kati," the Senator responds, rubbing his foot up Kati's leg. "She's just a product of the times."

Kati pulls off her pantyhose, sighing with relief. "She's certainly a product. She's been all over the place, who knows what she really thinks by now."

"Do you actually know her?"

"Not really."

Rupert Beveridge, columnist for The London World Chronicle, weighs in with the thought that people are tired of political ads so the President's bankroll may not overcome "voters' perceptions that he's in way over his head."

"Hope so," Wilson Burnett says. "Exactly why with all the Americans with opinions do we need to hear it from a Brit? They have their own problems."

"He was at Oxford, you know, and apparently seduced one sweet thing too many, and she blew the whistle when he dumped her. So they made a deal, he quietly left for The London World Chronicle which shipped him off to Washington. Anyway, she's fucking him."

"Lauren? And Beveridge? How do you know all this?"

"Read The Ear. You're surprised? He's not bad looking, in a dissipated and disheveled sort of way."

Lauren Baxter pushes her hair off her face as she cuts to a commercial. "And that hair's not real. Must take two hours to style it. Minimum. And to get out the gray."

"Meow," says Burnett as he rubs Kati Case's back. She unhooks her bra and tosses it on the floor with the pantyhose.

He *is* a nice man, Kati thinks, a lot nicer than I am. It's good to have an involvement based on more than lust. Her mind flits again to Brandon Jarrett. She shuts it down and asks where they should order dinner from.

*   *   *

Earlier, Amber Burnett, previously Amber Rice, actress, originally Alice Rosenfeld, waves Wilson Burnett off to the airport and leaves the rambling Toluca Lakes two-story for the Malibu beach pad. She opens the window so she can hear the surf. The breeze is early-

Spring chilly and damp, so she lights a fire, opens a bottle of Cabernet, and puts out two glasses.

Alice Rosenfeld. Yearbook Description: Most Popular; Yearbook Prediction: Star of the Cinema. Eliza Doolittle at Brookline High, reclusive Laura in The Glass Menagerie at NYU ("see, I can play against type"). And then, to the dismay of her lawyer father and professor mother, she quit college and migrated in the opposite direction from Lauren Baxter. With a new name, new golden hair, and eventually, implants, small parts came her way, occasionally with a line or two. Her biggest splash was in bed, boob job on display, with James Bond, only to be offed before the title ran by an electrocution device in the mattress, activated after 007 luckily left to take a piss.

Her big break came when Wilson Burnett, an ascending young Production officer who eventually rose to Executive V.P., sat down next to her in a Studio cafeteria and was pleasantly surprised to find she could make coherent conversation about topics ranging from the mess in the Middle East to the Golden Era of Broadway musicals. Tall, prematurely graying, and handsome as the actor he aspired to be but lacked the talent for, he became her ticket to a starring role: wife of rich studio honcho.

Amber also believes that Wilson Burnett is a nice man. She is, however, dismayed when, as she puts it, he's "roped into" running for the Senate, and, worse yet, wins. With her children inexplicably off to the frigid Midwest (her daughter, first an undergrad, now an M.B.A candidate in Ann Arbor, her son a film major at Northwestern), exceedingly affluent, and finally free to take full advantage of Southern California's weather and things to do, the last thing she's interested in is Washington's chilly winters ("I'm forever scarred by January in Boston") and malarial summers. So she makes clear to Wilson Burnett that even if he goes, she pretty much stays.

She and Kati Case have been together on several occasions and, modern woman that they are, manage to get along. It's as if they're French. It's my doing, Amber figures, that he's in Washington by himself, and it's better with Kati than if he hooks up with bimbos and brings home some disease. In another life, Kati Case could have been a friend.

To her knowledge, until now he's been about as faithful as you can expect, considering the amount of hot items that chase after a desirable Studio higher-up. And she's had her own dalliances.

"I could have been you," she tells Kati one time, melancholy after three Margaritas. "I'm rich and comfortable and all I've accomplished is a boob job, which I have to get rid of now anyway before my tits hit the floor." Kati tells her she's still attractive in her fifties, has raised two smart and beautiful children, etc., and changes the subject.

Before long, Roland Henery drops by. A genial character actor who knows Amber since their B-movie days, now he's relegated to flaky-grandpa roles and commercials for annuities, back spasm meds, retirement communities, and the like. He pre-dates Wilson Burnett, and, given what he knows about the Burnett's marital situation, wonders if he might post-date him as well. "Good to see you," he says as he gives her an affectionate peck on the cheek.

She fills the second wine glass, sits back down, and sighs.

"Everything OK?" he asks.

"Nothing new," she answers.

"You know, I'm here for you."

"Yeah. I wonder about that. Why? You've been chasing me for what, 30-odd years now, and what's it gotten you? And I just take advantage."

"That again? Look, like I said, I'm here if you need me, if not just tell me and I'll stay away. You're no kid, and I'm getting to be an old man. So *carpe diem,* they say."

"*Carpe diem,*" says Amber Burnett.

*   *   *

Wilson Burnett is somewhat revived, and he and Kati are sharing steamed dumplings, shrimp with black bean sauce, and Singapore noodles, along with another round of gin and tonics, in the dining alcove of her two-bedroom condo. Her second bedroom is set up as an office, but charitably includes a black and uncomfortable Ikea futon along one wall for the rare occasion Sam Jensen's in town. Kati is not much for décor, her walls are filled mostly with photos she's taken, many from a trip to Aruba with a long-ago boyfriend. A pelican landing on a pole; a wild goat behind a cactus in the desert interior; waves crashing on a black stone beach on the windward side; spooky divi divi trees with twisted trunks blown by the constant wind; seagulls. And a framed poster from Robert Kennedy's presidential campaign, a gift from her father on her first election to Congress, intended for her House office but which she prefers at home. Kati has a nice Canon DSLR and always carries a compact super zoom in her shoulder bag should something come along that she'd want to shoot. She'd like to take more photos, maybe do some classes, but where's the time? Sometimes it seems like it would be easier to be Amber Burnett.

"What's next?" he asks with a yawn.

"You announce Friday."

"What do I have to do?"

Kati scoops up a shrimp and some rice with her wooden restaurant-issue chopsticks. "Give the speech. Mike Bloom's finishing the first draft. Then I'll fix it. Keep begging people for cash. Look Presidential." Not a problem she thinks, he looks like central casting sent him. Which, in a way, is accurate.

"Do we have positions I need to be up on?" He puts more noodles on his plate, picks up a dumpling, dips it, eats it whole.

"Not really," she says, laughing. "Your position is that the President's an asshole. We'll put in some vague platitudes about how you'll be improving the world in every regard. Only take a couple of questions and get the Hell out of there."

"But don't we -- "

She cuts him off. "We'll put out position papers every week. About all the things you can do better than Bromwell. I have working drafts." She gestures toward her second bedroom. "But you don't need to see them yet."

"Oh -- Malcolm?"

"On board."

He gives a thumbs up and yawns again. "Bedtime, sweetie," Kati says. "Been a long day."

He goes to wash up while Kati puts away the leftovers. He's sound asleep while she's still brushing her teeth.

Chapter 14

EAR TO THE GROUND
By Roger Newley

The Presidential race is nearly here, and The Ear is listening carefully to keep on top of things. Contenders from every direction are moving toward the starter's gate, and this is what we're hearing about who's making the run.

Never in doubt, President Bromwell, 62, is running for re-election despite his pathetic approval ratings. Worse yet for him, The Ear hears from a very reliable source that internal D.N.C. polling has a Generic Republican defeating Bromwell by a whopping 50-42 in the popular vote, with only 8 per cent undecided, so there's widespread panic among Democrats.

As first reported by The Ear, California Senator Wilson Burnett, 55, will challenge Bromwell for the Democratic nomination. The word is that Senator Burnett will announce in front of the Capitol on Friday, saying he has been urged to run "to save the party and the country." His announcement, we hear, will be followed by rallies next week in Los Angeles and Philadelphia, where The Ear has been told he will have dual campaign headquarters. In an unprecedented move, The Ear's sources tell us that his running mate will be introduced in L.A.

But there's more. The Ear's eavesdropping has picked up rumblings that Randy Carraway, 41, a fishing guide and Mayor of Lakotah Lake, N.D. (population 24,328) will also toss a hat into the Democratic ring. Carraway, now in his first mayoral term, a former minor league hockey defenseman (6 goals, 421 penalty minutes in two seasons) who often makes public appearances without putting in his dental bridge, will describe himself as a Freedomtarian. No explanation so far on that.

On the Republican side, Utah Governor Rolf Baggett, 71, Indiana Senator Herman Marshall, 67, and South Carolina Governor Jefferson Butcher, 69, all have signaled they'll be running.

And listen to what The Ear also hears. Miami Mayor Guillermo Villar, 48, a Republican who has won two Miami-Dade nonpartisan elections, has scheduled a press conference for unannounced reasons in his hometown for next Monday. The Ear hears that he may be thinking of jumping in.

*   *   *

That was easy enough. Kati Case feeds him the Burnett news and the D.N.C. poll. Carraway -- a nut case? -- calls him up. The old Republicans have been sending out signals for months. Villar schedules a presser for no apparent reason, so Roger runs with it. It's worth a guess. If he's wrong, who'll remember? He sends it out, snacks on a bowl of Cheetos, and dozes off on the loveseat.

He has a Kati dream, wakes up foggy, restless, and horny. He takes a shower, puts on his usual khakis and a white button down shirt with red stripes, and makes some calls to firm up tomorrow's stories: a Justice investigation of bribes for FDA approvals of a diet drug pitched by a televangelist; and a staffer in the State Department hooking up with a Congressional intern. Work done, he decides to get out of the apartment and drive into Laurel to see if there's any action.

He heads for The Dugout on North Washington Boulevard, in a strip mall that for some reason otherwise specializes in glass: eyeglass repair, auto glass, auto glass tinting, home window solar tinting. The Dugout has decent tacos and burgers, drinks that aren't too watered down, and 19 gigantic screens so he can watch the Wizards and Caps at the same time -- unless something more interesting turns up. A night, he later reflects, that could be said to change the course of history.

There's nothing much doing at the bar. Happy couples are scattered around at tables. Depressing. He orders a blue-cheese-and-bacon Burger with fries and a Frozen Coconut Margarita as he watches the 70-inch screen on the wall a few seats down. The Wizards are getting blown out by the Sixers. He wonders if Kati's going to rag him about it.

A pretty and rather petite young woman, maybe mid-twenties, walks in, looks the place over, and in a definitive move takes the seat next to him. Roger Newley, although a bit overweight and with the pasty look of someone who's rarely outside, has a certain floppy-haired, puppy dog charm that many women find attractive.

"What's that?" she takes no time in asking, pointing at his drink. He pushes his hair off his face and tells her. "Looks so good," she says. Actually, he happily thinks, so does she. She waves the bartender over and orders one.

Things have certainly taken a turn for the better. She has strawberry hair and green eyes, and she's very pert. Maybe five foot two, which is OK, he's no more than 5'9, only an inch or so taller than Kati Case. Light green sweater and tight faded jeans. Twenty-six, he finds out, eight years younger than he is.

"Hey," she says, "I'm Marybeth Moran, I always thought it's a dumb name, but what can you do, I just broke up with my boyfriend, like two weeks ago, he's a personal injury lawyer, an asshole I stayed with way too long, I work as an IT in the White House, down underneath," she laughs, "the only time I see anyone is when something gets fucked up or some douchehead can't figure out how something works."

She talks a lot, and fast, he figures he'll know her life history by the second drink. This is good, because Roger himself is not much of a conversationalist, and he can't really get a word in anyway.

"I'm really such a nerd," she continues, "I'm never going back to Erie, dreary Erie the mistake on the lake, yuck, I knew I wasn't going back the day I got accepted at MIT."

MIT? He finally gets a chance to tell her his name. "I know you -- you're the guy who writes The Ear? I love it, you should put in even more about people hooking up, I thought you were some old guy, but actually you're cute. I wish I could write but it's a challenge for me to even write a letter, all I can do is computer stuff. I love classic rock, by the way, can you believe it, it's from like 50 years before I was born, well maybe not 50, but it must have been so cool then, I'd have been a hippie for sure, or a groupie, I'd have run off with Neil Young. And my ex is such a dickwad. I play in this softball league, I play second base, I'm pretty good, you'd be surprised how far I can hit for a little bit of a thing, I was on the team in high school, it was Catholic school and I hated it, my parents get annoyed that I never go to church anymore, and anyway, he'd come to games and just sit there reading his legal shit."

The bartender pushes her drink and Roger Newley's food across the bar. She takes a sip. "That's so yummy. The Wizards suck," she resumes, pointing at the TV, "they could at least try to play defense, if they can't play man try zone, the coach is an idiot. So what's going to happen in the election, I'll bet you know, I guess I'll have a job regardless, nobody cares about us, it's not like we're into politics, the one from California is really good looking, although I'm not really into guys that old."

She orders nachos and scarfs them down. "I'm little but I have a big appetite. And I don't gain weight, which is so cool." They have another round, then another. She's holding his hand. He's ignoring a pretty good game between the Caps and Bruins. She's not paying attention to the Wizards anymore.

"You should take me home now," she says. "I don't live very far. I'll drive. I'm Irish," she laughs, "I'm just getting started."

Her apartment is small and spotless. He's glad he isn't taking her back to the ratty den he lives in. She closes the door, gets on her tiptoes and jumps him, her tongue is heading for his tonsils. "Am I too aggressive, I'm kinda horny," she announces. He's not protesting. She walks him into the bedroom, pulls off her sweater and bra in one motion, slides down her jeans and panties.

She has nice round breasts, more full than you'd expect from such a small girl, and a hard tight ass. Very active in bed, there's obviously some things she can do besides computer stuff. After Meredith Simmons, he feels like he's hit the lottery.

Chapter 15

The cherry blossoms, in full pink riot outside the Oval Office, are lost on the occupants. The President of the United States sits behind the Resolute Desk, dog on lap, brown fur shedding profusely on his dark blue suit. Lanny Feldbaum, short but somewhat stocky, disappears into an enormous green leather chair to the right of the desk. Neither has much concern for nature's wonders blooming outside.

"That shithead from Hollywood's really running?" the President loudly spits out. "It's enough I have to deal with all the Republican fuckers, it's treasonous to get it from a Democrat." Startled by the noise, Artie turns and slobbers on his face. "Good boy, such a good boy," the President tells him. "You're the only one who's nice to Daddy." He pulls out a comb and runs it through his neatly clipped brown hair.

Lanny Feldbaum picks up a bust of Lincoln from the desk, one of the many pieces of Illinois memorabilia the First Lady has decorated with, and rolls it in his hands. "You look fine," he says. "That hockey player, he's running too."

"Thought he's a fisherman. Don't give a crap anyway, mayor of some jerk town in Minnesota or somewhere. Ridiculous."

"North Dakota."

"Worse yet. Like four electoral votes."

"Three."

"Republicans always win there anyway. What do we do about the movie star."

Feldbaum puts the Great Emancipator back on the desk. The First Lady is fair-minded, a portrait of Stephen Douglas is displayed on the wall along with Adlai Stevenson, even though, the President complains, they both lost. "We need to fill up the space with Illinois things, dear. We can't hang a picture of Blagojevich. Or Michael Jordan," she tells him, "even if you'd like to."

"I'm thinking of giving Mr. Movie a call," Feldbaum says. "Set him straight. Tell him about certain negative implications."

The President of the United States closes his eyes, pyramids his hands under his chin. Thinking? "Don't know that it's appropriate. You going to the candidate himself. A Senator. Your official position being somewhat obscure."

"You want to do it?"

"Fuck no. What about some high up in his campaign. Who's that?"

"Maybe Case."

"The Chief Justice? He can't do that."

"His daughter. The Congressperson, or whatever you're supposed to call her."

The President farts. The dog jumps off his lap, runs around the desk, and bounds onto Lanny Feldbaum. "The skinny one from Pennsylvania?"

"Yeah. Pretty, too. And screwing Burnett."

"Yes!" The President shouts. "That we can use."

"Can we? With all that ass we got for you back in Chicago. Then in Springfield. You think we can afford to get in the dirt? Don't think we can go there."

A long Presidential sigh. "OK. Call her. Give her some advice. Her career in Congress, you know. The Hollywood asshole probably doesn't give a shit, he can go back to making movies, but she might worry. By the way, what's with that General who was pissing around?"

"Don't know what you're talking about," says Feldbaum, standing up. "I'll call the little bitch. Go get on the treadmill, I hear you put on two more pounds."

Lanny Feldbaum walks down the hall to his office. A true fucking miracle that he's here in the West Wing. Two years at Roosevelt University, but never much for being a student, then dropping out when his father, after thirty-odd years of three packs a day, got the lung cancer diagnosis. Years of sharpening up his street smarts working for Ernie Pulaski, used car salesman, loan shark, bookie. Until Daniel Bromwell, who needed someone with balls he could trust, got in touch with his old school pal and took him along to the top.

*   *   *

"Kati, Lanny Feldbaum for you."

"Oh Jeez. OK."

"Good afternoon, Representative."

"Yes."

"Hear that you're involved with Senator Burnett."

She hangs up.

"Feldbaum again?"

"Well. OK."

"Representative, we must have been cut off. I was saying the Senator appears to be thinking of running for President, and you have a significant role."

"And?"

"We need to talk about it."

"I assume you're calling to let me know that Bromwell will do an LBJ."

Silence.

"Excuse me?"

"Step away gracefully since it's clear he lacks public support, is unlikely to be nominated, and would surely lose in November."

"You're fucking crazy, bitch."

She hangs up. Slimeball, bag man, fixer.

"Feldbaum. Want to take it?"

"No. But I will."

"Look, I'm just trying to give some advice. Friendly advice."

"Doesn't sound like either."

"Look. You're young, plenty potential. Whole career in front of you. The Senator, nice situation, why fuck it up. You run, he gets his ass whipped, you're forever on the shit list. He's making movies again. You, back in art school or whatever. Guaranteed."

"A threat?"

"Advice."

"And the dead horse in my bed? Don't forget -- "

"Look, you fucking stupid twat -- "

She hangs up.

"If he calls again, tell him I've left for a hearing."

Chapter 16

Ways and Means is considering increased subsidies for wheat farmers, suffering as more and more people go gluten-free. Kati Case, a logical choice for the prestigious committee assignment considering her Wharton Economics degree, is not particularly sympathetic to Midwest farmers who always vote Republican, but isn't categorically opposed. Malcolm Douglas, Chairperson, history major with a Master's in Education, both from Howard, gavels adjournment. Brandon Jarrett, on the committee because his father-in-law pulled some strings to make sure he has someone to watch over his money, scribbles on paper inside a notebook during the hearing. A crossword puzzle? Kati wonders.

He looks like he wants to talk with her, but Malcolm Douglas pulls her aside. "Drink?" Brandon Jarrett mouths. She shakes her head no. She has plans.

"Been thinking," Malcolm says, looking around to make sure the room has cleared. "I don't think I should be there Friday."

"Because?"

"It should be exclusively the Senator's day." He opens his collar, pulls down his red striped tie. "I'd be a distraction." He smiles. "The Senator can say he's introducing his running mate next week at the L.A. rally, make it so folks can't wait to hear. I'll be with him in Philly, too, and then I'm in Cleveland myself next weekend. It rolls out better that way."

"Sounds smart," Kati says. "I'll tell Wilson, he'll agree." She grins. "You're pretty good at this politics stuff, Mr. Douglas."

"I should have some sense after all this time," he chuckles. "And you too, Ms. Case, especially for a youngster."

*   *   *

"What do you know about Feldbaum?" Kati Case asks Carter Howell as they sit at his usual table at the Benjamin Rush.

He shakes the ice in his gin. Kati nurses a Bloody Mary. "Bromwell's guy? Nothing in particular past what everyone knows.

Divorced, a couple of kids back in Chicago, fiercely loyal to his boss, totally untrustworthy for anyone else. No scruples. Why?"

"He called me before. First, intimating about me and Wilson. Then just pretty much threatening me."

"No shock there. Exactly how?"

"Just about the end of my career. And Wilson's. 'On the shit list forever' or something."

"Utter nonsense. Reagan didn't do so badly after challenging Ford. Kennedy couldn't unseat Carter and went on to a career that put him in the top rank of Senators in history. I thought you were going to say he mentioned a hit man."

"Odd you should say that, since I did say something about a horse in my bed."

His rack of lamb, her salmon with olives and capers, arrive. "But Feldbaum's a particular prick."

"Look Kati, it truly goes with the territory. And so what? You're as safe as possible in your CD. I suppose they can primary the Senator when his seat's up, but again, so what? He's wealthy, they'd be thrilled to have him back at the Studio, even higher up than before. Ignoring crums and degenerates, it's part of the job."

"Crums and degenerates. I like that. You get off the phone with him, you feel like you need to disinfect it."

"And Malcolm. He certainly can take care of himself. There's hardly anyone in town who would think they could take him on." He forks a chunk of lamb. "Ah, delicious. One of life's remaining pleasures. "

Kati Case doesn't surprise easily, but she's pretty shocked. "You know about Malcolm? How?" She scans the nearby tables to convince herself it's safe in Howell's booth.

Sly smile. "Heard it. Somewhere. No worry, it's not really out there. Things do find their way to me still. He took some persuading, I suppose, not what I would expect him to want."

Her mind quickly skims through possible leak points and draws a blank. Except for Malcolm himself. As established as anyone in town, he's still asking Carter Howell for advice? And Carter telling him, yes, it's what you should do? Trust Kati, go for it? She can see that.

"Did you have to talk Wilson into it as well?" he asks.

A question that goes right to the heart of things, doesn't it? Do you think, Kati Case, that Wilson Burnett has burning ambition to be President? Does Malcolm Douglas need to leave his comfort zone in Congress? Kati Case, isn't this all about you? Yes, Wilson would clearly be better than Bromwell, and you could move him the right way on issues. That's the point, it's what *you* can do. Getting past where your father went, beyond where Lenore was able to push him? She shoves it out of mind. "He feels he should do it for the good of the country," is all she rather stiffly offers.

Carter Howell knows when it's time to change the subject. "I had the oddest discussion with a student today," he says.

"How so?" She gets some fish, capers and an olive slice onto her fork.

"We're covering Teddy Roosevelt, and he comes up to me after class, going on about the McKinley assassination, which I'd really just skimmed past. Odd little fellow, not even a full-time student, he apparently just takes classes while he works at night. Short, quite a bit shorter than you, shaved head, painfully thin, wears round wire rimmed spectacles like John Lennon had. Maurice Barry, or Barry Maurice, I forget. And the strangest part, then he starts in on Guy Fawkes and how the two are connected."

"Guy Fawkes and McKinley? What's one got to do with -- "

"Exactly. I told him that McKinley's assassin was a rather deranged anarchist, while the Guy Fawkes plot to blow up Parliament was almost a century earlier, in England, and had to do with putting a Catholic on the throne. There's no equating them."

"And?"

"And then he tells me that I don't understand because 'you've been part of it for years' or some such. That he grew up in northern Maine, 'away from all this' he put it, and his mother wasn't even American, so he has insight."

"Nice day," Kati says. "I get Feldbaum, you get this guy."

Chapter 17

At 11:25, Lanny Feldbaum turns on the 70-inch ultra high def Oval Office TV, whose main purpose is for watching the Cubs when they play in the afternoon.

"Do I have to watch this shit," the President grumbles.

"Back home, folks say a person needs to keep a keen eye on what the other guy's doin'," offers the Vice President, Clement McWillis, an innocuous backbencher from the Arkansas Senate who generally comes to the Oval Office only when a ball game is on. The Vice, bald and pink, weighs at least 260 and allows the President to claim his own weight is OK. McWillis is Vice President because of a typically futile effort by Democrats to gain some leverage in the South, and due to the President's need to have a running mate who wouldn't make him look bad by comparison. "The Vice Presidency has a long history of bein' obscure and not havin' much to do," he tells shocked associates when he agrees to be on the ticket, "and I surely can fit the bill."

Rupert Beveridge opined one evening on the Lauren Baxter Hour that this could be the most incompetent pairing in American history. "He's some limey," McWillis laughed, "if they're so fuckin' smart, how'd they lose the Revolution to a bunch of hicks with squirrel guns?"

The Vice President at 77 is not intending to re-up for another run, but only the President and Lanny Feldbaum know this. "Wait 'till just before the Convention to find someone else, see what we can get for it," Feldbaum advises.

TruNews goes live outside the Capitol, where Wilson Burnett has moved behind a podium draped with the mandatory flag. Wavy gray hair sprayed in place, chin firmly set, he stands alone. Kati Case is out of range, hanging out behind various aides and assistants to make sure no cameras pick her up. Malcolm Douglas is tuned to MSNBC in his office.

"Just another pretty boy," Lanny Feldbaum says.

"Beauty and the Beast," says the President. "And I know my part. Speaking of Beauty, where's the skinny bitch? Nice job you did with her, tough guy."

"You try next time," Feldbaum answers.

"The Case girl? That little one's pretty as a rose with spring raindrops on top," the Vice offers.

Wilson Burnett is starting to speak. Kati Case has pared the speech to 10 minutes. Dark eyes riveted forward, he sounds Presidential, just like she told him. Forceful without raising his voice, he spends five minutes calmly summarizing Bromwell's failings, with Iran in a starring role; and five more describing without detail how things will be better when he takes over. Finally, he teases the Vice Presidential pick set for Monday in L.A. as a "great American who has devoted his career to his country and who represents the broad diversity of the Democratic Party."

"A Schvatsa?" Feldbaum wonders.

"Can't go usin' words like that, you know," McWillis scolds.

Burnett takes two questions.

First, he recognizes Roger Newley, primed with a softball provided by Kati Case: "What's your vision for America?" The Candidate spits out a well-rehearsed response that will become part of every rally, predicting peace, prosperity, income equality, freedom from crime, safety from disease, and fair treatment for all.

Second, Mimi Sellers, MSNBC's White House correspondent, a safe pick, asks a bland question about the "daunting prospect of a primary challenge to an incumbent." The candidate flashes a movie star grin. "I have supreme confidence that the wisdom of the American public will prevail." He waves to the cameras and leaves.

"Didn't say a fucking thing," says the President of the United States.

"Looked pretty doin' it though," say the Vice with a chuckle. "What he's all about, ain't it."

"Little bitch must've written it," says Feldbaum. "Probably programs his brain while she's giving him blow jobs."

"That kind of talk ain't right," says McWillis.

* * *

By 11:55, Wilson Burnett is on his way to the waiting campaign plane -- white with blue striping, BURNETT in red lettering and American flags on the side -- at Reagan National. Away from the cameras, Kati Case slips into the backseat, and, well pleased with his performance, plants a wet kiss. Specially cleared, it's wheels up at 11:25. With an office in the rear that's fitted out for her, she sits by herself reworking the rally speech while The Candidate jokes with aides up front, then goes back to see how she's doing.

He stands behind her, massaging her shoulders. "Nice," she says, so he keeps it up, looking over her shoulder at the text she's playing around with.

"Should I be doing more?" he asks.

"I'll be done before we land. I'll forward it."

"Sometimes I think I'm just the front man here."

Kati stops typing and turns. He takes his hands away. "Fact is, I'm the detail nerd, the policy wonk, whatever. The more you want to get into it, fine, Bloom and I could use the help. But it's not like you should be doing something you don't want to. You're an executive, that's what you've been, that's how you operate. You're good at it, you're great giving the speeches. So if we keep our lanes, that's OK too. And you can go rub my back some more."

"It's just that sometimes I wonder, why I'm the candidate. Not you."

"Because you can win. I'm 37. Nobody knows me."

His fingers dig into the tight muscles around her neck.
She sighs, momentarily contented.

"I'm sorry you're stuck in a hotel for the weekend while I get to go
home," he says.

"Yeah, right, I could take the guest bedroom," she laughs. "Amber's big about this, but there's a bridge too far."

"Wasn't suggesting -- "

"Just kidding. Next week you're invited to stay at Pine Street. Let me finish this. It's tricky. Don't want to go too heavy on details that only the other nerds will listen to, but you need to say . . . something."

"Got it." He heads back to the front.

With only mild headwinds, they're on the ground at 2:35 p.m. PDT.

*   *   *

After meeting with the guys who'll be running the cyber campaign and the ad agency that's handling their media spots, Kati Case is in her room at the Marriott adjacent to L.A. Live where the kickoff rally is scheduled. The room has a gigantic bed which she'd like to share, but that's not happening, pale yellow and blue carpeting that's very SoCal, sufficient work space, and a view to the mountains which are passably visible through the brownish haze. There's nothing much out here that Kati likes (except its Senator), all cement and strip malls punctuated by palm trees which don't give enough shade, her eyes burn when she's outside for long, and pretty as everyone says she is, she feels intimidated by all the very blonde, oft-siliconed women. "It's like my hair's too dark and my boobs get an inferiority complex," she complains, but Wilson Burnett just laughs.

Malcolm Douglas calls her from LAX. To keep the secret, he and Glenda didn't get on the campaign plane. They arrange to get together the next day to go over his speech.

Her phone buzzes again, Brandon Jarrett's name is on the screen. She hesitates, then takes the call.

"Hey, sweet thing," he says. "Where you be?"

"L.A."

"L.A.?" Man, you move fast. Guess we're not getting together."

"Didn't think we were," she says, maybe too nastily. Fact is, she's getting a little tingle between her legs, which she pushes aside.

"Watched the announcement. Nice job."

Kati realizes they don't have a lot to talk about. "Sorry, but I'm really busy here. Nice of you to call."

"Yeah. Right." He sounds kind of disappointed.

Off the phone, she looks a bit sadly at her comfy bed, then gets back to work.

*　　*　　*

Lauren Baxter leafs through staff research on Randy Carraway, scheduled for today's program, as her interminable hair groom proceeds. Running for President, and we're dignifying it? Lord, what has it come to?

Somehow mixed in with the papers is a letter on notebook paper addressed to "LOVLY LARREN AT TRUNEWS" which has managed to find its way to her. The envelope is dirty, the writing in smudged pencil. Likewise the message inside:

Ma cherie LARREN
Je t'aime, je t'aime, je t'aime. Je vais te le prouver.
Votre adorateur.

Jesus Leroi

She hated French in college. She chucks it in the trash and goes back to Carraway.

*　　*　　*

Marybeth Moran calls. "Roger, you're all over TV. I loved your question. Out of all those reporters, he picked you out. See, people know you're good. I want a Coconut Margarita. I want you. Like really bad. Get down here. Like right now."

Roger Newley complies.

*　　*　　*

"This is the dipshit fisherman?" asks the President of the United States. "Why do we need to be watching this?"

"He's running for President. You're running for President. See the connection?" says Lanny Feldbaum.

"Don't be snotty. She's hot."

"Baxter?"

"Not the fisherman. Who's going to vote for this dick?"

"The 64-dollar question. The unwashed and the disaffected? Not a small group. Maybe he gets enough delegates to keep you under 50 per cent and then the convention's a shit show."

"I hear she's screwing that pompous Englishman."

"Pay attention."

"I am."

"To him, not the pussy."

"Yeah, Yeah."

"There's always the superdelegates."

"Yeah. I thought he didn't have teeth."

"Guess he puts them in for special occasions."

"There's something I'd like to put in that Baxter woman."

"How about you go have dinner. I've got this."

"Yeah. Remember, Bulls at eight."

*　　*　　*

Kati Case rummages through the minibar, finds a little green bottle of Tanqueray, plops in a few cubes from the ice bucket, and settles down to watch the West Coast recording of Lauren Baxter's handling of the Burnett announcement. It goes well enough until Baxter's concluding comment that "Judging from this kickoff, we can expect the Burnett campaign is going to be not much more than 'I'm smoother and a lot prettier than Bromwell.' He is, after all, a bit of a manufactured candidate. So next, we'll give you an alternative approach, the Mayor of Lakotah Lake, North Dakota, Randy Carraway."

"Bitch," says Kati out loud, particularly pissed off that trotting out Carraway deflects attention from Burnett. "Bitch, bitch, bitch."

Carraway is on. He has shoulder length reddish hair, almost as long as Lauren Baxter's. Wearing a blue and black plaid flannel shirt and ratty looking jeans, he could pass for homeless.

"Mayor Carraway," she starts, "thanks for coming."

"Anytime," he says, and doesn't hide the fact he's looking her over, focused particularly on her blue sweater that matches her cornflower blue eyes, although it's not her eyes he's checking out. "Pig," says Kati, continuing the discussion with herself, "and she's as flat-chested as I am."

"Mayor, I want to start with what I know everyone's asking. You've been Mayor of a small town in North Dakota for two years. A part time job. Your experience is as a fishing guide and minor league hockey player."

"And not a very good one," he interrupts, "but won almost all my fights. Had lots."

"Yes. So how with your background do you figure that you're qualified for the Presidency?"

Randy Carraway pulls out a purple handkerchief the size of a small towel and blows his nose hard enough that Lauren Baxter jumps back in her chair. "Look Ma'm, we're tired of politicians who make money, money folks can't dream of, running things. The jerk in the White House is lifelong getting taxpayer money and anyone can see doesn't know his ass -- can I say that?"

"It's cable. Go ahead."

"Doesn't know his ass from a Milky Way bar."

"Huh?" says Kati.

"And the other guy, he has a fancy house in California, a place in Malibu, a condo somewhere in Washington, who knows what else. How's he relate? Tell me that. They pay me six grand a year to be Mayor, I make maybe thirty thou more taking people fishing, and some more plowing snow in winter. I know what it's like to eat canned beans for a week 'till there's some cash. And then I have to stay out of public pretty much, with all the farts I blow."

Kati, despite herself, laughs out loud. Lauren Baxter looks like she's wishing for a trapdoor under his chair. She soldiers on. "But to be President?"

"I'm telling you, lady, it's getting things done in the real world. Ben Randolph got the flu during a two-foot snow, I had to do all mine plus his to clear the way to the state highway. So there. And this daylight savings crap. Every year, people bitching, clocks forward, clocks backward, can't remember which is which. Politicians say let's do something, and nothing happens. First day in the White House, that's history."

Lauren Baxter rolls her eyes. "So your campaign is about plowing snow and daylight savings?"

"You could say that."

"Foreign affairs?"

"Screw them all. That's what we all say back home. That's what folks think, down inside. I-ran. Is-re-ale. Let them figure it out."

"OK. So finally, you describe yourself as a Freedomtarian. Can you elucidate on what that means?"

"Can I what?"

"Explain."

"Yeah. No fifty buck words, lady. Anyway, isn't that what I just did?"

Lauren Baxter looks relieved as the voice in her earphone tells her it's time for a commercial. "Yes. Well, we need to take a break. Thank you, Mayor."

"Sure." He pops out his teeth.

Even Kati Case feels some compassion for Lauren Baxter.

Chapter 18

Still on East Coast time, Kati Case is awake at 5, showers, throws on jeans and a faded gray Penn sweatshirt, and orders half a cantaloupe, an almond croissant, and a pot of coffee from room service. She fires up her IPad for a leisurely read through the New York Times, London World Chronicle, L.A. Times, Chicago Tribune, Miami Herald, and what's left of the Washington Herald. She finishes with the Philadelphia Inquirer, where she allows herself the luxury of the sports section.

By now it's late morning in Miami. Guillermo Villar comes in from the backyard of his Mediterranean villa in Coral Gables after playing catch with his 13-year-old son, an aspiring pitcher. On the short side and heavyset, with unruly black curls and a bushy mustache, Guillermo Villar was himself a catcher back in the day, and still has his old mitt.

He pours himself a glass of lemonade and reviews the day's news just like Kati Case is doing 3,000 miles to the West. The elderly and pale-faced Republicans will be easy picking, he believes, largely indistinguishable and likely splitting votes, leaving him to be a self-proclaimed dose of "fresh air and diversity for a party in desperate need." If he's correct, he'd prefer to run against Bromwell, an unpopular buffoon and a far more assailable candidate than the slick and handsome, if a bit plastic, California senator. Carraway has no chance, of course, but is nonetheless intriguing. There's a market out there for the outrageous, and the Villar campaign can take advantage of that as well.

Guillermo Villar is in his second term as Miami-Dade mayor. No dummy, he astutely picks his issues, hires competent people to run things, and maintains a constant presence. A fire, he's on the scene, praising the courageous firefighters. A murder, he consoles the victim's family. A hurricane, he's at a destroyed house, picking a child's teddy bear out of the rubble. The streets flood, he paddles along in his kayak. And in Miami, where it really counts, he's professionally Cuban and "one of you."

He pulls it off while speaking at best rudimentary Spanish, being married to a Jewish emergency room physician -- which he's sure to make known to the retirees on the Beach -- and living in near palatial splendor in one of the County's most upscale neighborhoods. His grandfather, a superior ball player to Guillermo, was out of Cuba well before the Revolution, made it to the majors, and after a not particularly distinguished career, took his earnings and invested well in car dealerships. His own father was a wealthy orthodontist, his mother a very successful real estate broker. His brother's an attorney, his sister a physics professor at Georgia Tech. All that's left is for him to be President.

*   *   *

Mike Bloom and Kati Case are debating whether to resurrect a wealth tax proposal while they wait for Malcolm Douglas to drop by. He would like to. She would too, but worries that it's going to drive more money to Bromwell and scare some Burnett contributors.

Mike Bloom and Kati go all the way back to the Rittenhouse Square neighborhood where they grew up two blocks apart and walked together many days to their Friends school in town. Bloom is tall and thin with dark curly hair. An Orthodox Jew who tries to keep Kosher, he's pretty much confined to tuna salad and the like on the road, which now is most of the time. He excuses himself to call his husband back in D.C., an analyst at Brookings where they met, who's recovering from gall bladder surgery.

In a prepubescent fantasy, Kati imagined marrying Mike Bloom when they grew up. That ended at 13, when she mentioned that she thought Jason Timberlake was the kind of hot guy she could like, and Bloom said so would I -- the first time he'd ever told anyone. He was the valedictorian, Kati was third in the class but had better SAT's, he went on to Columbia, then to the Kennedy School for his Masters, Kati turned down Harvard much to her father's distress to go to Wharton.

"We live a boring life," Bloom once told her, "we go out to dinner, we go to the movies or the theater, we stay home and watch a ball game or old Law & Orders."

"You're the most angst-free person in the world," she said.

"Well if you combine you and me, you get one average person on the angst scale," he replied.

He was excited when Kati was elected to Congress and wound up in Washington most of the time. Little did he know he'd wind up taking leaves of absence at Brookings to work on presidential campaigns she seemed intent on masterminding every four years.

Malcolm Douglas is there when Bloom returns. They go over what he'll say, a condensed version of his standard campaign speech, shortened for the occasion so as to not upstage the presidential candidate -- a difficult proposition because he's well known as a powerful speech maker.

Back to the wealth tax, they ask his opinion. "Look at the realities now," he says, "you're on Ways and Means so I don't need to tell you what it takes to get stuff done. And then to pass it on the floor. And get it through the Senate. Maybe someday. But what I say is, you don't lose an election over something you can't get passed anyway." End of discussion.

They leave Kati drowsy and alone. Wilson Burnett calls. Sitting by the rectangular pool in front of a rose bush, going over his speech, he offers minor suggestions. He'll come by tomorrow morning for a run through. He asks if he should score courtside tickets for the Clippers game for her and Mike Bloom, he's tight with the owner. "Sounds good," she says. She wonders if he and Amber are doing it.

The Governor calls. Kati doesn't know her. She's introducing the candidate on Monday, flying in from Sacramento tomorrow. Wants to have a drink with Kati at 6.

Hoping for a perk-up, she goes for a walk. Nobody knows her here, no one turns as Kati Case goes by. Just another pretty thing in a town full of them. Younger ones, too. She stops for sushi, passes on the exotic varieties you can't get back East and just gets her usual salmon rolls and tuna rolls.

She tries to work after lunch, but her eyelids droop. She considers calling Brandon Jarrett, thinks she was too curt yesterday. But he must be at home with his wife, or out golfing. Instead, she rents a movie, and watches until Mike Bloom calls from the lobby, ready to head over to the Staples Center.

* * *

The Candidate stands by the window, rehearsing his speech. Kati, dressed like she's 16 in cutoff denim shorts and a white Phillies t-shirt with blue sleeves and red lettering, is perched on the bed. He seems distracted, stumbles where he should be hitting high points. She stops him. "It's just another speech. You've given hundreds. Start over and get focused."

He turns and takes in the view. In white slacks, dark blue cloth belt, lighter blue polo shirt, and white tennis shoes, every gray hair in place, he looks very much the handsome and affluent middle-aged Californian at brunch time.

"There's a difference, you know," he answers finally, turning back to her and sounding annoyed. "The stakes. The hype. Trying to be leader of the free world. Until I got into all this, I only had to worry whether to green-light another Emma Stone project. So -- "

"So?

"Did your Dad have misgivings when he ran?"

She stops to think. "Not that he ever said. Lenore started him on the road and he just followed it."

"And you took over. And now, here we are. Isn't it pretty much the same thing?"

"Oh please, give me a break," she answers, raising her voice. "You're thinking you're a father figure? I still have one of those, remember? Fact is, everyone knows it, I'm just a power-crazy witch. So just do the damn speech."

He looks sheepish. "Sorry." He does another run-through, much better this time.

"Yes!" Kati congratulates. "See. All you needed was a little push from the witch."

He puts his notes on the desk and sits down on the bed. She moves closer, puts her head on his chest. He's still in shape, works out, runs a few miles most days, he's not so middle-aged after all. He runs his hand up her leg, to her bare thigh and beyond. She takes off her shirt, she conveniently hasn't bothered with a bra, her little nipples are already on the alert. They make love, sweetly, like they always do. Not with the lightning bolts Brandon Jarrett gave her, but that's fine.

* * *

Juanita Gomez, a slight fiftyish woman in a black pantsuit sits across from Kati Case in the lobby bar, she with a whiskey and soda, Kati with Beefeater and ice the way Carter Howell taught her to have it. The lobby has large rectangular gray panels with white dots hanging from the ceiling and reflecting off shiny black tables. Annoyingly space-age to Kati's taste, she's the child of a hundreds-year old city on the other coast. Now wearing a white sweater and khaki-colored slacks, she's surprised at how unimposing the Governor looks and how little of a stir it seems to make that she's there. In a city where running into the larger-than-life is commonplace, what, after all, is another politician.

"So," the Governor says, "I've heard a lot about you."

"I'll bet," Kati responds. "I hate to think what."

"What they say is smart, ambitious, aggressive, hyper-focused, stubborn. And a ball-buster."

She laughs. "Yup. Compliments, aren't they, if I also happened to have a penis. And?"

"And is why I wanted to get together. Senator Burnett has been very supportive. I owe him, you could say. It's why I'm introducing him tomorrow. And I figured you, you're going to be in the line of fire too, take it from someone who's been."

"Yeah. I'm ready. I hope."

"Sure. But, you know, you're often not ready as you think. Imagine, a little Latina lesbian whose father put three kids through college running a Bodega in West San Jose, becomes Mayor, then Governor. Lots of rocks on that path."

"Bodega? My grandfather has a corner grocery in South Philly."

"Really. I thought you were straight Main Line."

"Only my Dad's side. My Mom was Lenore Cardelli. Grandpa, Pop Joe, he drove a delivery truck and saved up to buy the store. It was his dream, now everyone in the neighborhood stops in, to buy stuff, but mainly just to shoot the shit. The Mayor of 6th and Reed, they say."

"Your mother. She died young, yes?"

"Car crash. All those things they're saying about me, that was her. In spades."

"By the way. I know all about your husband."

"Really?"

"It gets around. Among us. And it's just a matter of time before it's out."

Kati shrugs. "His problem."

"Maybe. Well, just take it from me, I don't know I have that much to offer, but just this: when the rocks on the path look too big, walk around them. Jump over. Whatever. So long as you go forward."

Back up in her room, Kati googles "Juanita Gomez Wilson Burnett." The primary wasn't bad, the general election got nasty. GOP-allied holy bloggers called her "Wetback Pervert." Internet ads said "Keep California Straight and Anglo." And then, there was a TV ad with Wilson Burnett -- Juanita Gomez and her wife standing beside him: "This isn't the California I know. This isn't the California where I grew up. This isn't the California where Juanita Gomez grew up, where Juanita Gomez is the distinguished mayor of the largest city in Northern California. Look at accomplishments, look at ability, ignore hate, and vote for Juanita Gomez for Governor." She won with 56% of the vote. Kati smiles. Good for you, Wilson Burnett.

Chapter 19

Lenore's driving the gray Audi, Kati's riding shotgun. "Law School makes the most sense. Period," Lenore says loudly.

"I want to get an M.B.A., a Ph.D. Maybe I want to teach. I don't want to be you. Or Dad," contrary Kati yells back.

"Get over it. You don't know what you want."

"Fuck you."

The car swerves in the dark. Airborne. Trees ahead.

Kati bolts awake. Wide awake. 3 a.m., in a Los Angeles hotel room, and she's staring at the ceiling.

This is hardly the first time for Kati to dream she's arguing with her mother as Lenore's car crashes. A shrink would have a field day. And she knows what happens next: there's no chance of getting back to sleep, everything starts to re-run.

I am, she thinks, really my mother's creation. Maybe that's what the dream means. I'm just a ball-busting witch, even Wilson's starting to pick up on that, it's all about me, me, me. Did I really mean it, that I wanted to just settle down in some quiet college town and live like a normal person. Am I capable of that? Probably not. What have I ever done that's consistent with something like that? But I still think about it.

She remembers sitting in her car seat as they drove down Pine Street toward Jefferson Hospital, with Lenore in the front seat holding a towel turning crimson. There's going to be no little sister, Lenore later explained, and the doctors had to do some things, so there won't ever be one. What would it have been like to have a sister, Kati's often wondered. How different would I be if there'd been someone else around, so I didn't just go to my room to plan, and scheme, and imagine, when I got home?

She hears spattering against the window. Wearing maroon boxers and the black Iverson jersey that's her favorite piece of sleepwear, she gets up and sees that indeed it's raining. Apparently out here it's allowed to rain at night. She goes back to bed.

She pictures the back seat of a car by the beach. "Are you a --
?" the boy asked. She doesn't recall his name. She can pretty much
remember what he looked like, though. "Yes," she casually answered,
like it's no big deal. So there's another towel, on the seat so the blood,
Kati's blood, doesn't stain the fabric. He went home two days later, to
start soon at Brown. He wrote to her, and she started to write back, but
she couldn't think of exactly what to say and let it drop. Back in school,
next to Bloom at weekly Friends Meeting, Kati whispered "I got laid
this summer, should I get up and say it?" He rolled his eyes. Mike
Bloom is her oldest friend. Her only friend? Too bad I don't have
girlfriends, she thinks. Neither did Lenore.

She thinks back to when she was a community organizer --
which she managed to fit in when she wasn't working on her father's
career -- to the Resident at Jefferson and the cute quarterback from
Purdue with the great body who tried to make the Eagles, got cut after
training camp, and wound up on ESPN. And the bright young lawyer at
the big downtown firm she went to Aruba with, holding hands, taking
photos, and watching the sunset. When Carl Billings was indicted, she
said she was going to run for his House seat. So she'd be in
Washington a lot. He's married now with a pretty wife, a couple of
kids, and a seven-figure house in Villanova.

And, of course, her Junior year, second semester, when she met
Robert Crawford -- a nice boy, handsome, decent -- at a frat party
where she'd been fixed up with some football oaf. She found her way
to him instead and gave him her number. God, they were crazy for each
other. The bed creaked in his seedy West Philadelphia apartment, they
wondered if his roommates in the living room were laughing. He went
rock climbing that summer in Utah, fell and died. She cried for days
and days, maybe more than for Lenore. It makes her teary still. Was
that her chance, lost to fate? Or just a memory, a dream preserved in
amber, because it never had a chance to end like all the rest.

With her hopeless marriage finished, while her husband was
slipping pretty boys into the Statehouse in Concord, she went for a run
in Rock Creek Park, and this handsome older guy jogged up behind
her. I know you, you're Wilson Burnett, she said as she looked over
her shoulder. And you're Kati Case, I know who you are too, and do

you think it's safe for you to be out here alone? Then run with me, she said, and you should ask me for dinner later. Late last year, Amber told her, "He's in love with you. Do you want him?"

"He is? And what about you?"

"It's alright I suppose. Life's one accident after another, you just move along and wait for the next one."

"Let's see. After the campaign."

How annoying is this, she thinks, I can't sleep and what's going through my mind is all these damn men. Like someone once said, they're like streetcars, another one comes along in a minute.

Brandon Jarrett?

Chapter 20

In a town where it's imperative to not let anyone know what you're thinking or planning, and where nobody can keep a secret, it gets back to Lauren Baxter that Kati Case doesn't like her. This bothers her on a personal level, and is professionally disturbing since Kati is someone who's likely on the way up and is therefore a person Lauren needs to be connecting with.

It's not like I've ever said anything bad about her, she thinks, and anyway, I say nasty stuff about people all the time, and around here they know not to take it personally. I don't remember even meeting the woman, except maybe across the room at some party I couldn't wait to leave.

Like when I said Burnett's a manufactured candidate the other day. Big fucking deal. She's the one whose manufacturing him, everyone knows it. That's why she's interesting. Fact is, we should be girlfriends.

She turns on her TV to watch the Burnett rally and find out who's the running mate.

*   *   *

It goes like clockwork, just the way Mike Bloom organized it.

Rasul Gerritsen, the Los Angeles mayor, looks out over Xbox plaza, which he's made sure is available, at the crowd he's made sure would fill it up, praises the Candidate and introduces the Governor.

The Governor praises the Mayor, describes the virtues of the Candidate, and introduces Wilson Burnett, who thanks everyone and brings out "the most qualified Vice Presidential candidate in history, Malcolm Douglas."

Malcolm Douglas, voice booming, invokes Dr. King, John Lewis, three Kennedy's, Barack, throws in Kobe, and reintroduces the next President, Wilson Burnett, who will restore the Democratic Party, and our country.

The Candidate, demeanor highly presidential, with the Microsoft Theater to his right and surrounded by black and yellow LA Live towers, nails the speech, which he'll give, with minor modifications that pander to local interests, close to a hundred times before the primary voting.

Kati Case, relieved as much as elated, is looking forward to a couple of days home in Philadelphia.

Chapter 21

"What's with you and that Kati Case, are y'all fuckin'?" Andrea Weatherill Jarrett asks after too many Bloody Mary's and too much wine. The Georgetown townhouse décor, unlike at Fairfax where the glories of the old South are abundantly displayed, is modern. The walls are covered with abstract art her designer overpaid for, and that Brandon Jarrett doesn't pretend to understand, with stalky light fixtures that look like they belong in Han Solo's apartment.

"Where's that coming from?" he answers, sounding shocked.

"You talk 'bout her a whole lot. The way she whores around, makes sense."

"She's on Ways and Means, I'm on Ways and Means. So is Annette Tannehill. You think I'm doing it with her?"

"That's just stupid. Annette Tannehill is like 70. You're not that desperate."

He tries to be conciliatory. "Look, Kati Case is an intelligent young woman, a very talented Rep. We work together. And I don't really see that she's 'whorin' around.'"

"Not what I hear."

"From?"

"Around."

He sighs. "Listen to yourself."

She can be a teary drunk. "You should fuck me more. That'd solve the problem," she sniffles.

"Fine with me."

"And if it's that Kati Case, if y'all's fuckin', Daddy's gonna cut your balls off."

Like he hasn't already, Brandon Jarrett thinks.

Chapter 22

Alton Road in South Beach is thigh high in King Tide flooding. Two wooden platforms, one for the speaker, the other for the assembled press, stand in the middle of the closed off street. Guillermo Villar makes his entrance, paddling up in a kayak.

Helped up a ladder, he raises his arms in triumph, waves at the TV cameras, looks away and waves some more in every direction -- although no one's around -- and begins to speak.

"Thank you, my friends, gracias amigos. Today is the start of the redemption of the Republican Party and of our nation.

"Let me introduce myself to all you folks who need to get to know me. I'm Guillermo Villar, the mayor of Miami-Dade County. I am a Republican elected in non-partisan elections in a strongly Democratic County. I win not because of my party, but because of who I am, and my ideas. Today, I announce my candidacy for President of our great nation, great yes, but also in great need.

"The Republican Party in our nation is frozen in time. It can no longer continue to be a party of old white men with old thinking. Our nation is spiraling downward under the leadership of a Democratic president unfit for office, challenged now in his own party, but only by others who promise more of the same. Where, I ask, are the exciting ideas that made America?

"As weeks pass, you will hear in detail what my ideas are. Today, I offer examples of the revolutionary thinking we need.

"First, look around. My city, slipping underwater. What has the government of the United States done to help us in South Florida? Nothing. Endless debate over changing climate, taking away our cars and gasoline, restricting our air conditioning so the vulnerable will die in the heat, making our lives more miserable still.

"No, I don't accept that. No, no acepto eso. Enough talk of changing the weather, the weather is made by God. Dios haco el clima. I propose not to fight the Lord, but to work with what he has made. So when I am El Presidente we will institute a nation-wide program, in

Florida, in South Carolina, in Texas, in California, in Manhattan, everywhere, to build sea walls and dikes, the time-honored way to cope with what the Lord has wrought. We will stop the water, and we will put people to work, we will create thousands and thousands of jobs.

"Now another thing. I am proudly Cuban. Soy orgullosamente Cubana! My grandparents were born on the island, they fled for a better life. But now the Castros are gone, God be praised. It is time to invite all Cubans to a new and better place, to unite the Cuban people. Para unir pueblo Cubano. So on my first day in the White House, I will proudly open negotiations with the government of Cuba to become our 51st state, and in this, I am sure I'll succeed.

"These are fresh ideas you haven't heard before. I have many more, and I look forward to sharing them with you. Thank you and have a wonderful day."

The press shout questions. He ignores them, climbs down into the kayak, and paddles off.

In the living room on the second floor of the 19th century townhouse on Pine Street where Kati Case grew up, sitting on the gray sofa that's been there since her parents bought the place, Wilson Burnett rolls his eyes. "Did that really happen. Or is it jet-lag?"

"We don't need to worry about him for the time being," Kati, seated next to him, says, "but he sure seems on the crazy side. We've had a pump in the basement here all along, there was a little lake down there when we moved in. Maybe we should've just built a dike."

Mike Bloom is sitting in an upholstered rocking chair to the other side of the TV on which CNN now is covering growing tension in the Mideast. "I'm not so sure how crazy he is. My guess is he doesn't believe a word of that bullshit. He's supposed to be astute enough politically, he wants to carve out a niche."

"Does it affect us, do you think?" The Candidate asks.

"Only to the extent it maybe gives a lunatic like Carraway more credibility," Kati offers. "If off-the-wall is the new normal, he's right there."

"Hadn't thought of that angle," Bloom says. "Could be."

"So being sane is no advantage?" Wilson Burnett says. "And I used to think the directors were nuts."

Chapter 23

PRESIDENTIAL CAMPAIGN: CHAPTER ONE
Rupert Beveridge *in Washington for The London World Chronicle*

Now that the United States has joined other civilized nations in limiting the duration of its Presidential campaigns, we can provide an analysis in a more sensible manner. Or as sensible as it can be in an American election.

And this one promises to be the kind of Wild-West event that only our American friends can produce. At the kickoff, four Republicans are in the race, while, in a stunning development, two Democrats will challenge the beleaguered incumbent, Daniel Bromwell. Today, we look at the Democrats.

Under attack from all sides, Bromwell is defiant. "I'm no quitter, I've never lost an election, and I'm not about to start now," he said yesterday in a brief appearance on the White House lawn. "The candidates who are challenging me for the nomination are blindly ambitious but totally unqualified. A senator whose main claim to fame is producing B movies. And a fisherman. I was the Governor of one of our largest states and have kept a steady hand on the national rudder as President. I'm confident American voters know me and support me." Bromwell took no questions after his statement.

Bromwell has the support of significant elements of the Democratic establishment and is reputed to have a massive war chest for the primary and the general election. However, in a composite of the first primary polls taken since the candidates announced, he stands at only 38%, a shockingly low number for an incumbent.

Wilson Burnett, Senator from California, is the main challenger on the Democratic side. Burnett, a former Hollywood studio executive, has a reputation for moderate views, not making waves, and being easy to work with.

In another surprising turn, Burnett has already picked a running mate, 10-term Ohio Congressman Malcolm Douglas, a leader of the Congressional Black Caucus. Sources that wish to remain anonymous say that if Burnett can consolidate the African-American vote, especially in southern states where Black voters constitute large majorities in the Democratic primary, he could be on the way to a large delegate accumulation.

Despite suffering from far less name recognition than the President and having no clear image, Burnett is on 32% in early polling, well within striking distance of Bromwell.

The wild card in the race is Randy Carraway, a fishing guide and part-time mayor of a small North Dakota town. Carraway, who left high school after two years to help with his family snow plowing and lawn care business and to futilely pursue a career in ice hockey, describes himself as the "real person that we need," whatever that may mean. The only position he has presented is opposition to moving the clocks from standard to daylight savings time and back.

In what insiders describe as "stunning" Carraway is on 16% in the opening poll composite. Sources surmise that Carraway's standing reflects a deep well of disaffected voters who will get behind any candidate viewed as outside the lines. Although there seems to be no scenario by which he could prevail, if Carraway maintains or increases his standing, he could have enough to swing the nomination should he support one of the other two candidates, or deadlock the convention.

And keep in mind, 14% are now undecided.

In our next story, we shall look at the Republicans.

*   *   *

Rupert Beveridge files the piece. He feels a headache coming on, leans back in his desk chair, closes his eyes, and rests his hands over his face. He's a disgruntled man, an Oxford Don exiled at 62, turned into a hack writing about American politics. "This is what comes of thinking with your dick, Rupert old man," he remembers Sandy Blake laughing in the faculty lounge. But isn't the sentence rather harsh? It's not as if it were rape, she asked him to sit beside her on his office sofa, batted her big black eyes, and queried with such a charming smile if the stains were coffee -- or semen. She wondered, sitting so close he could smell the shampoo she used, if Henry in truth waited all that time for Anne Boleyn. How, really, she said, sighing, could any man be so patient?

Why would she think she was different from any of the others, that it somehow would last forever? Did she honestly think he'd marry her? She was surely of age, it's not like the damn-fool Prince with his arm around a child who should be at a Sweet 16 party. Perhaps a censure, not the sack, not shipped off like a disgraced Padre who fiddles with the choir boys. So here he is, typing out garbage about this bizarre election. We had Boris, but he's Eton and Oxford, not like this lot. A buffoon in the White House; a movie producer (at least he was an executive, Reagan just acted, and not all that well); a high school drop-out; a Cuban who wants to build dikes. I should interview the pretty Case girl. I wonder what Lauren thinks of her. He opens his eyes, looks at his watch, and heads off to her place.

*   *   *

Lauren Baxter, who's become rich from being a TV star, lives in a white 4,000 square-foot two-story on a cul de sac in Bethesda, with a pool and a hot tub; gleaming hardwood floors; a gourmet kitchen with maple cabinets and granite countertops which the housekeeper, who picks her 10-year old son Jordan up at school, cooks in; a large rec room in the basement for the boy to play in; and a home office for her.

Gourmet kitchen notwithstanding, tonight Rupert Beveridge is treated to take-out pizza (part of becoming American?) and a Newcastle Brown Ale which she keeps on hand for him (part of attempting not to?), before they put Jordan, one of the only remnants of her long-defunct marriage, to bed.

They share Grand Marnier, her choice although he finds it rather on the sweet side, and discuss what he should write about the Republicans. She finds Villar interesting, if nothing else, far-removed as he is from the Republican she was raised to be and once was. The others are so "stiflingly dull," she says, insisting Villar should be his focus.

They make sure the boy is sound asleep and repair to the bedroom. She finds the lovemaking perfunctory, "he's English after all," she tells a friend. He rarely stays the night, it's difficult enough to get the child off to school.

Rupert Beveridge opens her front door and a gunshot explodes in the quiet suburban night. The bullet ricochets harmlessly off a tree, perhaps ten yards away. He dives back inside. The police arrive, after much flashlighting around, retrieve the bullet, drive up and down through the neighborhood finding nothing, and go back to the station to write it up. Rupert Beveridge decides to spend the night after all.

Chapter 24

Nine at night in Tel Aviv, where Yitzhak Kohn, deputy director of Mossad, Collections, the intelligence unit, is just starting a meeting with Andrew ("Chip") Chester, on the books as an American embassy employee but in fact CIA.

Kohn, a man with a perpetually perturbed look, and who can blame him given his job, is particularly pissed off. "So?" is all he says.

"So nothing, sorry to say," says Chip Chester, a slender man of medium height with heavy black rimmed glasses and a short haircut, who carries himself with the pacific demeanor of someone who spends time calming agitated Americans who've lost their passports and had their cameras stolen.

"I don't understand, not one bit, how this can happen, and how, after all this time, you don't know how," Kohn yells.

Chester shrugs. "What we know is that somehow the White House thought Iran would attack, we don't know why, and authorized a military action, and somehow Iran found out, we don't know how."

"Which is what you knew, or didn't know, when all this started."

"Can't deny that. The White House is completely clammed up, and there's only so far you can go with them, and every lead we've taken on the leak dead ends. So -- "

"Your President -- "

"Isn't very smart and is running for reelection, so he'd like everyone to forget all this happened, which isn't helping."

Kohn runs his hands through his curly red hair and scratches his matching beard. He leafs through the stack of reports on his desk, picks one out, and slams it on the table. "And look, now we're hearing that Tehran *is* up to something. But no one can do a thing about it, because it's crying wolf, we get told. All because of the mess you made."

"I'd love to be more help. Really. We're still on it. Of course, if we find out -- "

"Great. Great," Kohn spits back. "We're done. I have hours more here." He picks up a folder from the pile.

"Always a pleasure, Yitzhak," says Chip Chester.

Chapter 25

Carter Howell comes down with pneumonia, so Kati Case postpones her surrogate speech in Boston and instead goes to Medstar Georgetown to visit. He's sitting up, laptop on the tray table, when she walks into his room.

He brightens noticeably. "Kati Case, what in heaven's name are you doing here, not out on the campaign trail?"

"The question is, Professor Howell, what are *you* doing here. You look pretty good to me."

Not really. He's paler than usual, and drawn. She tries to put aside the thought of losing him.

"Good enough to hop into this bed with?" he asks.

She gives him the finger. "You old piss-ass, you're fine."

"I just have a touch of pneumonia, actually, nothing very serious, but at my age everything is a crisis, so they've been keeping me here for a bit. I should be out in a day or two, then I have to take it slow for a week or so."

Kati fumbles in her shoulder bag, takes out a plastic Dasani bottle and an insulated thermos with ice. "Medicine," she says, grabbing a plastic cup from the bedside table, dropping in two ice cubes, and then pouring from the water bottle. "Sorry it's not chilled. And you can't have too much."

"Is that what I think it is?"

"What else?"

"The Jesuits running this place don't know where true sainthood lies."

"Hah," she says. "Saint Kati? Patron saint of juniper berries? Not something I have much chance at. Anyway, there's more." She reaches back into the bag and produces a very rare sirloin burger with onion rings from the Benjamin Rush.

"A veritable Demeter among mortals," he says

"Excuse me?"

"Oh. Greek goddess of food. You need to brush up on your classics."

"Do I now. You should see what it took to get the BR to do take-out. I used some words that weren't very saint-like. But they relented when I told them who it was for and why."

"So how goes it?" he asks, after a bite of burger, an onion ring, and a sip of gin.

"OK I guess," she says. "With the campaign condensed the way it is now, you're on the road all the time. Wilson's out West with Bloom, Malcolm's in the Midwest, I'm in the East, I think we've got Governor Gomez somewhere. The thing is, nobody knows who the hell I am, just some obscure Rep, so I go on the evening news and I spend half the time explaining what I'm doing there."

"But think. By the time it's done, you'll have a national profile, win or lose. You're quite young you know, it surely will stand you in good stead down the road."

Kati walks over to the window, stares out. "But to what end, really?" She drops into the hard-gray visitors' chair. "I already wonder -- "

"Yes. I know, I know. They tried to get me to run for Governor in New York, a great many years ago. I turned it down, I lacked the personality for it, I suppose. But you, you walk in and light up a room. Don't be discouraged. You're just tired, I'd say."

"And I'm going to be more tired. I rescheduled Boston to bring your care package, and then I'm swinging through New Hampshire, Vermont, Albany, Syracuse, Buffalo. I wake up in the morning and I don't know where I am. Wilson says they have to remind him just before he makes a speech what city it is. Insane. I did this four years ago with my father, and here I am again. Why is that? I mean, would Wilson have done this if I hadn't pushed? I'm not so sure even I get what I'm doing. What I'm after. Who I am. And the thing is, I'm getting kind of tired of being me. I'm 37 and I'm already burning out. I'm sorry, I shouldn't be laying all this on you."

"Well who better? I've heard it all before, you know. And introspection, I find, can be useful, if you don't let it carry you away. Anyway, what reaction are you getting out there?"

She shrugs. "Pretty positive, I guess. But who knows. We're running against an incumbent who has tons of money, he's on the air and the web all over the place while he hides in the White House and acts like he's running the country. I guess they figure the less people actually see him, the better off he is."

Carter Howell reflects, continuing to work on his burger and gin. "What are you picking up out there on this Carraway person?" he asks finally.

"A mystery. Nobody you talk to admits they're for him, but some people seem to be giving him money, and he's polling at close to twenty per cent, even more in some places in the Midwest. I don't get it."

"Rupert Beveridge wrote something about how the disaffected don't care who it is, as long as the candidate is disaffected too. He may have something. He thinks it applies to Villar as well."

"That reminds me. Do you know Beveridge?" Kati asks.

"I do, actually. Met him when I was in London, when he first got into trouble. He's quite intelligent, but he's an angry man, feels quite put upon. Why do you ask?"

"He wants to interview me. I'm afraid he'll do some nasty power-behind-the throne story."

"Any publicity is good publicity they say. Anyway, just smile, he's still a sucker for a pretty face, I'd bet." He finishes the gin. "Refresher?"

She nods no. "We're in a damn hospital. Be thankful for what you've got."

"Can I ask you something? Besides another drink."

"Sure."

"If you're still in town tomorrow, how would you like to teach my class. I've been having friends fill in while I'm stuck here so it doesn't just fall apart. But they're over-the-hill geezers like me. They'd love to have you."

"I'm in town. But how -- ?"

He points to a textbook and a stack of handwritten notes on top of the radiator. "Just read the chapter the night before, and there are my lecture notes. Feel free to tell your own jokes and make it less boring.

They're usually somnambulant, but if they ask questions, make up an answer."

She isn't about to turn him down.

She leaves. He has great hopes for her, this young woman, remarkable in her way. Perhaps ordinary in others? Or is she just an old man's final infatuation? For her, there will be so many twists and turns. Who knows what her path will be. As flies to wanton boys are we to the gods, he thinks, surprised he still remembers that. He will not, he suspects, be around to see what happens, which makes him a bit melancholy.

*   *   *

Despite countless public appearances, and innumerable speeches, Kati Case is singularly nervous about standing in front of a classroom of 30 or so students and trying to get through Carter Howell's lecture notes. She spends the better part of an hour picking through her closet, figuring out what to wear that won't be too formal, or too casual, finally settling on black jeans, a plain white blouse, and a navy linen blazer. She walks into the classroom and is met with bored indifference, with the assumption that after a series of the professor's superannuated buddies, they're getting a grad student.

She tells them who she is, a celebrity of sorts, and they perk up. The boys, the straight ones at least, like the idea of an hour of eye-candy in the front of the room, and begin to work on major crushes; the girls want to be her. I was once young like that, she thinks. Toward the rear she notices an older, bald little man with John Lennon glasses, the guy Carter told her something about, she can't recall what.

Harry Truman is the subject, an accidental President the lecture notes put it. After reading the textbook, reviewing Carter Howell's notes, and going to Google and Wikipedia, Kati, who didn't know all that much about him, has discovered that before suddenly finding himself President when FDR inconveniently died, he apparently was content drinking bourbon and playing poker with his pals. The notes contain a quote, Truman to reporters, which Kati dutifully reads to the class: "Boys, if you ever pray, pray for me now. I don't know if you fellas ever had a load of hay fall on you, but when they told me what happened yesterday, I felt like the moon, the stars, and all the planets had fallen on me."

And then she decides -- hoping she's not screwing up -- to take the chance of going off script, to ask what they, the class, would think, would do, with the weight of the world suddenly dropped on their shoulders. "I'm a city girl, I've never been hit with a bale of hay," Kati Case says, "and I bet you haven't either. It's 1945 and you're Harry Truman. Put yourself in his shoes. What's it like? What do you do?"

In particular, they want to talk about the incomprehensible choice of dropping atomic bombs on Japan rather than invading. At one point, a young woman in the third row surprises her by asking, "Ms. Case, you've been elected to Congress, tell us what you think you would have done."

"That's a great question, and the answer is, I don't have a clue," she responds. "So since I can't answer the damn question myself, maybe I was an asshole for asking it."

They laugh. They like her. The class is over so quickly, she hasn't made it all that far in Carter Howell's lesson notes. She worries he'll be upset. But several students, engaged, come up after class to ask more questions, to continue to debate. Finally done, Kati packs up the textbook and notes, and realizes she's enjoyed it more than anything in quite a while.

Chapter 26

Rupert Beveridge plays around with his Irish briar pipe, and, stupendously bored, tries to write his column about the Republican presidential candidates. He keeps getting the three old white guys confused, and finally decides, screw it, it'll just be a profile of Villar.

He finds himself even more at loose ends than usual since experiencing the particular American pleasure of being shot at. A stray bullet, the cops conclude, somewhere in the neighborhood some asshole trying to shoot a raccoon that's keeping him awake rummaging through trash. He's not so sure. How then did the bullet manage to find its way to Lauren Baxter's tree, scant yards away, just as he exits her front door? Lauren is a pleasant diversion, but truth be told, not enough to get gunned down for.

Hasn't this gone on long enough? Has enough time passed for Oxford to take me back? Or perhaps I could swallow my pride and apply to a lesser institution. Or ask the editors for reassignment to home. Not that America is all that bad. The folks are generally congenial, at least when they aren't opening fire. There's functioning heat when it's cold, air conditioning that works, thank God, for the enervating summers if you're stuck in Washington, and the plumbing operates reliably. And if things have begun to deteriorate, if America's time on top of the world seems to be ending -- look at this year's political prospects, for example -- things are far better than for a largely irrelevant island off the coast of Europe.

He begins to write but stops, dissatisfied with what he has. He misses the days when he could show his disgust by angrily ripping a sheet out of his old Remington and tossing it in the trash can. Tapping the delete key isn't nearly the same.

Back at it, he pontificates about American malaise, the decline of the Yankee spirit, the vacuum of leadership, the rise of the disaffected. Blah, blah, blah, a horse he keeps beating long past its demise but they love it back in London. Villar, he goes on, is a desperate attempt by the Republicans to find relevance in a world that's changed while they dozed, even if his supposedly fresh ideas make little sense.

The reality is, he writes, Villar gives them a road to the presidency that the others lack. With the growing Spanish-speaking population in Florida, Texas, Arizona, Nevada, and in major cities elsewhere, he can bring in a demographic the Republicans need. Once you get past the crazy stuff that serves as an attention-getter, but little more, he's conservative enough to keep them happy.

So, Rupert Beveridge predicts, early as it is, Villar it will be for the GOP. Not that anyone cares what I have to say, he thinks, as he reads it over. But in London, they like it when he goes out on a limb.

Chapter 27

Randy Carraway is on his way to check out how his boat has survived winter when his phone buzzes. He doesn't recognize the number. Finally, he decides to answer anyway.

"Carraway?" says an unfamiliar voice.

"Yeah."

"Feldbaum here."

He doesn't know any Feldbaum. A Jewish name, it sounds like. He rarely encounters Jews, maybe once in a while they go fishing with him, but it doesn't seem to be something they're much into. "Who?" he asks.

"Lanny Feldbaum."

Maybe he's selling insurance? "Whatever it is, I don't need it."

Louder: "It's Lanny Feldbaum, I said."

"I heard that. Who are you, anyhow?"

"I'm in the White House."

"Yeah right."

This Feldbaum guy is beginning to sound annoyed. "You don't know me? I'm like the President's right hand guy. I was just in with him. In the White House. We just had lunch. Good burgers at the White House."

"Good burgers at the White Castle, pal. Stop shittin' me."

"Look here," Feldbaum's voice is rising again, "I'm serious. We need to be talking. Maybe there's something worthwhile in it for you."

Randy Carraway considers that possibly this guy is for real. The campaign is progressing and I'm now a national figure, he thinks. Who knows?

"So talk."

"What we need to discuss, you don't do on the phone. You'll learn."

Carraway laughs. "You guys are, I don't know what. Well, feel free to come on out. I'm just on the way to getting my boat ready. We'll go fishing. I'll give you a rate."

"We talk in the middle of the lake? Nobody around, right?"
"Just the fish."
"OK. I'll get back to you." He hangs up.
Randy Carraway shakes his head. For real? Unlikely.

Chapter 28

Seriously? Now you want to be a professor? And give up everything you've been working for? Don't go kidding yourself, Kaitlyn. You are what you are. Get used to it.

Thanks so much, Lenore. I've decided, I'm all your fault. Too bad you left before you finished the job. And you know, I'm really sick of it: she's so smart, so pretty, such personality. She'll go so far. Couldn't I be pretty, and smart, and not forever fend off guys trying to fuck me, and not always need to be the one with the right answer, and not constantly be faking the personality I'm supposed to have? Why can't I just go to work, come home, put on sweatpants and watch a ballgame, or even a cop show? Be Mike Bloom. Every night. Get laid if I'm horny. Or just do myself, it's less complicated. Answer me that.

That's gross. You're impossible, Kaitlyn, always were.

And why am I still hearing from you?

Chapter 29

Memorial Day weekend isn't far off, and Marybeth Moran wants to make plans. "I like the beach," she says, "we had a beach in Erie, out on Presque Isle, after they cleaned up the Lake, sort of, you could go in, but it's not like here, it isn't salt and there's no ocean smell, and you don't see shells and stuff. And there's this cute pink two-piece I saw, you'd like me in it. So maybe Ocean City, or Rehobeth, I think I like Ocean City more, there's more going on, or maybe even Atlantic City, I can hit the casinos and pay for the whole thing, and I like the buffets, but it's pretty far, especially with the holiday traffic, so I don't know. Maybe Ocean City. Although the water's still kind of cold, maybe it won't be that crowded."

They've just finished watching Harry Potter and the Goblet of Fire. "It's so sad when Voldemort kills Cedric, especially since he's so cute, Cedric, not Voldemort, I'm just a geek, I remember when I was little and my Dad read them to me, I wore a robe and a witch's hat and I had my Hedwig on my lap, and then I read them myself over and over, and I can watch the movies like that too, I wanted to be Hermione, I kept waiting for my owl to come, and you should see how well I do with Hogwarts trivia. It's part of the package when you get me. So." Sitting next to her on her couch, Roger Newley is idly fondling her left breast as she goes back to beach options. He isn't really big on the beach, or being outdoors much at all, but that's OK. "Sounds good to me," he tells her.

His phone rings. He reluctantly lets go of the boob. Kind of late for a call, maybe a hot tip? The caller identifies himself as General Evan Hurley, U.S. Army, retired. "Something I need to talk about. Something serious. Very serious."

The name is vaguely familiar. Pentagon? Roger Newley suggests a time, at his office. The General declines, he doesn't want to be seen there. He suggests three days later, at the Starbucks on Lee Highway in Arlington, at 8 at night when it's not too busy. Strange. And a long drive home for Roger, but a story's a story.

Marybeth is on TripAdvisor, working on Memorial Day in Atlantic City. "So if the weather sucks one day, there's more to do, and the drive's not really that bad, maybe we can get Friday off and beat the traffic on the way, and coming back, who cares if we get back late, you're just out of it at work the next day, big deal, right?"

"Right," he says.

"Good. I'll make reservations. Let's go to bed," she answers.

Chapter 30

Kati Case gets a phone call from Sam Jensen. It's their first contact in months. Since she's headed for New England, this isn't a big surprise. She's considered getting in touch, but hasn't quite gotten around to it. Or maybe hasn't really wanted to.

He's apologetic. Yes, he's heard she's doing great. Yes, he'd like to see her when she's in New Hampshire. Yes, Burnett is far superior to Bromwell. Yes, if he were a free agent, he'd support him. Yes, New Hampshire doesn't matter that much now that there's national voting and it's not the first primary, but every bit helps. Yes, there are times he really does miss her, but he suspects she's too busy for it to be mutual. But no, seeing as he's getting heavy-duty shit from the DNC, which Bromwell controls, and, remember, he has to run every two years in a state that's evenly divided, and he needs their money -- he can't endorse. The best he can do is stay neutral in the primary -- a hard-won victory just to achieve that -- and yes, if Burnett gets the nomination, he'll do whatever's necessary for November.

No point in arguing. Kati's long past expecting profiles in courage. Having a drink together would be nice, but she needs to get on the road to Burlington as soon as she's done in Manchester, she won't even be in Concord, so maybe some other time.

She does her meet-and-greets, rallies troops for some get-out-the-vote organizing, and sits down for lunch with a bunch of guys with money who want assurance that their taxes won't go up much. Begging is largely The Candidate's job, he has so many connections and does it effortlessly. Raking in contributions hasn't really been necessary for her congressional elections which are effectively uncontested, so it isn't something she's done much or is too keen on. But with the funding that's going to be needed for the primary and, hopefully, the general election, they're not about to rely on one of those grass-roots internet contribution efforts, so she pitches in.

Back on the road, up I-93, then I-89, the drive to Burlington is less than three hours, not worth flying. This entire swing is going to be by car.

Sheryl Sheldon is with her. On a leave of absence from law school at UCLA to help the campaign, Sheryl's a high school friend of Merrilyn Burnett. "Like a member of the family, I was always at their house," she informed Kati. Her assignment is getting Kati Case in to, and out of, wherever it is she's supposed to be, which at the moment means having google maps on her phone and doing the driving on this road trip, while Kati sits next to her and tries to work without getting carsick.

She was quickly informed when Sheryl Sheldon came on board that -- like a member of the family -- she knew all about what was up with Kati Case and Wilson Burnett. "Not a problem," she assured Kati. "I know Mrs. B. can live with it, and Merrilyn, I guess, although maybe not so much. It's the modern world, you know. So -- "

Sheryl's on the plain side, her hair's an in-between length that doesn't do much for her, and Kati thinks -- but doesn't mention -- that she should ditch her sea green glasses with the photo chrome lenses for contacts. She seems interested in Mike Bloom even though he's much older, until Kati sets her straight. And she seems so young. Because she is, I suppose, and I'm not anymore, Kati concludes.

Passing the Hanover exit, Kati briefly muses about a snotty boy from Dartmouth she was once fixed up with, but who didn't get to first base. The round-topped and aptly named Green Mountains are up ahead, looking better than the Hanover-Lebanon sprawl. "Oh shit," she abruptly exclaims, "get off at the next rest stop."

"Are you OK?" concerned Sheryl asks, thinking Kati's about to barf from trying to read in the car.

"I just got my fucking period," Kati says. She saw this coming, since she's been feeling like one of the giant balloons that go down Central Park West on Thanksgiving Day, but she's been hoping, irrationally, that perhaps the inevitability of her cycle would defer to the singular effort required to elect the leader of the free world.

"Got mine two days ago," Sheryl offers. "We're, like, on schedule. Had cramps, but not so bad."

Kati isn't all that interested in Sheryl Sheldon's menstrual experiences. Her own, other than some bloating, are blessedly mild, she just views it as an annoying pain in the ass. Reaching puberty both reinforced Kati's view that she'd rather be a boy and confirmed that it wasn't going to happen. It also motivated an obsessive interest in Joan of Arc. Kati had no interest in talking to saints -- although maybe her mother, and definitely Grandma Angela, would have been really excited if she managed it -- and she certainly wasn't anxious to have anyone set her on fire. But if she was going to be stuck as a girl, wearing armor and leading an army seemed pretty cool. Mike Bloom told her that it had some deep psychological meaning, but he didn't know exactly what.

*   *   *

Thoroughly bored, Kati stares out the window as they drive the East-West length of the NY Thruway, noticing nothing more interesting than signs about the Erie Canal. They campaign in Albany, Syracuse, Rochester, and Buffalo, ending up in a Hilton near the Buffalo airport. Tomorrow, she and her trusty escort will ditch the rental car and fly back to Washington. Or maybe Philadelphia? She's sure Sheryl knows.

She's working on a proposal to revitalize the Consumer Financial Protection Bureau when Mike Bloom calls from Minneapolis. "We have a problem," he tells her. "Amber has to have a hysterectomy."

A shitty week for the campaign's female reproductive systems, she thinks. "What happened?" she asks. "Is she alright?"

"I don't know the details. Not sure I want to. But the Senator's going to LA to be with her, so he's off the trail for a little while."

"Which means?"

"Which means you need to do Cincinnati next week. A rally and fundraiser both. They're big events, and you know how important Ohio is."

"Why me?"

"Douglas is in the South working the Black vote. Gomez is in Arizona, Nevada, and Texas speaking Spanish. You're it."

"How's Wilson?"

"Tired, but who isn't. He's still out tonight having dinner with millionaires. You?"

"OK. Working on Consumer Financial. We need a roll out soon. I'll email it if I ever finish."

"And we have to start working on debate prep," he mentions before hanging up.

She gets off and calls Sheryl Sheldon with the new plan. What's with Amber Burnett? Sheryl hasn't heard. Kati thinks about it for a while and finally decides to call.

"You've heard, I guess. I've been hurting and doing some bleeding," Amber explains. "Got an ultrasound, they think it's just a fibroid. Hopefully. But they need to operate."

"That sucks."

"Yeah, but could be worse, I guess. And, you know, whatever comes along is what you deal with. I told Wilson not to cancel stuff, but he insists on being here 'till I get out of the hospital. He's like that. So sorry, not great timing."

Kati forces a laugh. "You hardly need to be apologizing. So good luck."

"Yeah, thanks. And thanks for calling. I appreciate it. Really."

Kati sits quietly for a few minutes, feeling sorry for the world. Poor Amber, out in California, feeling crappy, heading for surgery, then weeks recuperating with some in-home nurse, why is she apologizing when her husband's running around the country and spending time in someone else's bed? Poor Wilson, is there any way he gets suckered into all this if the bed he's in isn't my bed? Poor Kati, who's beginning to feel responsible for all sorts of disparate events of an adverse nature. She goes to the minibar and finds a brandy to help unwind, puts Consumer Financial in the document bag that gets dragged around wherever she goes, and turns on the 11 O'Clock News. She sees herself for 30 seconds or so, mixed in with two fires, a murder, the weather, baseball scores, and reports on the basketball and hockey playoffs that she's completely lost track of.

Chapter 31

The Giant on Washington Boulevard, not far from the Arlington apartment he moved into when his wife passed on, is pretty quiet by nine at night, when Evan Hurley likes to do his shopping. He meanders the aisles, picking out instant oatmeal, 1% milk, sliced salami, a sourdough bread, a couple of steaks he can grill on his little patio, some frozen vegetables, TV dinners for when he doesn't feel like fussing, like tomorrow night when he's meeting that reporter. A weight off his mind, he thinks, when he'll get to sit down with him.

He wheels his cart into the parking lot and pops open the hatch of the gray Impreza. As he loads the groceries, a dark figure, hoodie up, slips out of a small car with Kansas plates, comes up behind him, removes a pistol, silencer on, from his pocket, and shoots General Evan Hurley, U.S. Army, retired, in the back of the head, then again to make sure. The assailant quickly pulls his victim's wallet out of his pocket, calmly returns to his car, and drives away.

Roger Newley finds out about it the next morning -- GENERAL ROBBED AND MURDERED OUTSIDE ARLINGTON GROCERY -- when he checks the news as he eats his usual breakfast of a powdered donut and coffee. (Although when he stays over at her place, Marybeth Moran forces him into something more substantial, some kind of organic cereal that looks like dog food with raisins and cranberries and other things the nature of which are unclear to him. "I eat so much crap, and some day I'm going to just have stuff that's good for you, but not yet, 'cause I like burgers and nachos too much, and I'm still pretty young, but for one meal a day I try to be healthier," she explains). Evan Hurley, that's the guy alright. Holy shit. He checks his calendar. Yeah, supposed to meet him tonight. Shot twice in the head, and some thug grabbed his wallet.

Surveillance video of the Giant parking lot is "inconclusive" the police say, which Roger Newley understands to mean they can't see shit. The dark car the killer used is an uncertain type, possibly a Corolla, and the Kansas plate is a fake. A witness, name withheld, from across the lot noticed only "two men coming together and one falling forward into the back of the car," but nothing much else. General Hurley's wallet is missing, the assumption of the police is it's a robbery, and the perpetrator panicked and shot the victim.

More than a little shaken, Roger Newley wipes sugar and crumbs off his pajamas and considers whether he has anything to add. It doesn't seem so. He has no idea what the guy wanted to talk about. In checking him out before their meeting, he discovered only that Hurley was assigned to the Pentagon for a while, and has over the years voiced some strongly conservative opinions, some considered racist, and definitely homophobic, and then retired not long ago. Likely I'm not the only one, he figures, the poor guy was probably all over the place venting right wing manifestos. The world can be a shitty place. He tries to think about something else.

Chapter 32

"To tell you the truth, things suck."

"Well Kaitlyn, aren't you the bright little ray of sunshine."

"Sorry. I'm just feeling kind of down."

"The campaign? It seems to be going well enough. Poll numbers are holding up, you're within the margin of error, although I don't know what to make of this Carraway character."

"I'm just tired. Of it, of whatever. Wondering why, you know, I do things."

"Isn't it usually because of who you are?"

"Is it? That's something I'm having questions about."

"And what things, exactly?"

"Just things."

"That's the best you can do?"

"Look. I'm traveling all over the place, pushing someone for President who probably wouldn't be doing it if he wasn't sleeping with me, and I can't really explain why."

"Maybe it's something you shouldn't do every four years."

"Well, there's that. But with you, I felt, you know, I had to. For Lenore. And you wanted it."

"At the end. By then I'd convinced myself the country needed me. The Senator, is that what he thinks?"

"More like he's convinced I convinced him."

"Your mother had to push me, you know. When I got into it at the beginning. I was happy as a prosecutor."

"If you think you're cheering me up by pointing out how much I can be like her, you're missing the point."

"You're not her. You're who you are."

"Isn't that where we started. Who am I? A monomaniacal witch is what people think."

"Please. Enough. True, I'm biased, being that I'm your father, but to me, you're inherently a very decent person. Smart and wanting to do the right things."

"Inherently. To my father. Otherwise, a monomaniacal witch."

"I give up."

"Look, this is what I'm thinking. One more term and I'm out of here. I can go back to school, get a Ph.D. Maybe Econ. Maybe PoliSci, I'd be really in demand there, I can get a nice teaching job. I taught a class of Carter Howell's when he was sick, and I loved it. So -- "

"One class? You'd get bored."

"'And 'you're cut out for bigger things, you need to maximize your potential,' right Lenore?"

"Yes. She'd say that. I sure heard it enough."

"'Suck it up, Kaitlyn, stop whining and get moving.' I can hear her now."

"Well, at this point, what's the choice?"

"None. I'm not giving up on something I've committed to. But still you know, that doesn't mean it doesn't suck."

Chapter 33

Wilson Burnett is sitting in a waiting room at Cedars-Sinai in West Hollywood, worrying about his wife. And paradoxically, also missing Kati Case, who he doesn't at all think is a monomaniacal witch. On his lap is a position paper on tax reform -- his position -- that she and Mike Bloom prepared, and that he needs to be signing off on.

He finds the detail pretty boring. A big picture guy, she called him. He comes from money, so he was free to satisfy a frivolous interest in going into movies by enrolling at USC to learn how. It turned out to be a successful and lucrative career, he only got richer. Politics, the Senate, wasn't in the plan until a group of friends, even more affluent than he, talked him into it. Being a senator isn't a bad life at all, the staff does lots of the work, he can advocate for worthwhile things, it's too bad he has to spend so much time in a place like Washington. You grow up in L.A., you don't really want to go back East. And it doesn't help when the wife absolutely refuses.

Never, of course, did he think about the White House. Who does? Maybe if you're born into politics. But he's born into investments and evolves into films.

His thoughts slip back to Kati Case. Amber says I'm in love with her. Quite possibly. But what's that mean? And who's to say I'm not still in love with Amber, even if she thinks I'm not.

The Doctor comes in. A Korean woman, youngish, around Kati's age. She smiles. Everything went smoothly. As we thought, a harmless fibroid. You can see her in a bit, we'll come get you. He thanks her profusely. She leaves and he resumes looking at whatever his position on tax reform is.

Chapter 34

Kati Case resolves to stop whining. She's in an upscale hotel on Fountain Square in downtown Cincinnati. Pricey for the campaign, but after staying in mid-range motels on last week's New England-NY Thruway tour, she deserves it, especially if it helps her to stop whining. The room is a bit odd, actually, starkly modern in some ways, with odd gray and black patterned wallpaper, but with a frilly bedspread that looks to her like it belonged to Marie Antionette. A fitting role model for me, Kati thinks. Then remembers to stop whining.

Another resolution is for Kati to have a little more down time. Instead of reworking position papers or drafting debate points until after midnight, she dismisses Sheryl Sheldon; chucks her bra and changes into a t-shirt and jeans; orders Turbot with mushrooms, ginger and soy broth and a half bottle of Chardonnay from room service; idly watches an NBA playoff game -- instead of the news -- while she dines; and thinks about renting a movie. She even considers turning off her phone, but her conscience prevents going quite that far.

So it's on when Brandon Jarrett calls. And reports, to her considerable amazement and dismay, that he's in the lobby.

"How did you find me and what the fuck are you doing here?"

"You should be a little more enthusiastic that I'm close by, sweet thing," he says and laughs. "Your whereabouts aren't classified, not yet, and my district is just over the river, remember? I'm back home for some constituent service, and I thought I'd stop by and see if you'd like company."

"And how's Andrea?"

"Back in D.C. She has some hospital fundraiser this week, or something. I know she'd very much appreciate you asking after her."

"I'm sure. Well thanks for the call, but I'm in for the evening."

"OK. I guess. I just thought. Well, never mind."

Just thought? She goes back to checking out movie options.

Against her better judgment, she's now distracted. She has a conversation with herself that's happened multiple times since That

Night. With everything else on your plate, Good Kati argues, the last thing you need is Brandon Jarrett. Good in bed isn't enough, he's shallow, phony, and living off his dumb wife's fortune. He makes zero contribution as a Congressman. And he's a Republican.

But man, was he a good fuck, Bad Kati answers. And you sure could stand to get some. Talk about needing down time. Stop harping on all his faults, he's not a bad guy at heart, we all do what we have to do. Who'll know? And man, was he a good fuck.

She can't find a movie she'd like to spend two hours with. He calls again.

Don't be a whore, Good Kati insists. When men do it, nobody calls them whores, Bad Kati responds. "Wonderin' if y'all might reconsider, sweet thing," he asks.

"Definitely not if you talk like a hick."

"I'm all Trenton, if that does it for you."

What does it for you isn't his accent, Bad Kati points out. Don't go whoring, says Good Kati, who's losing ground.

It's hard for her to ignore that her nipples are now quite erect.

"This makes no sense," she tells him. Right, says Good Kati.

"I don't think we're talking about sense here." He sounds more serious. "I'd like to see you, really I would. You're special, I always thought you were."

"Room 761." Whore, says Good Kati.

She lets him in. He closes the door and kisses her hard. Her t-shirt is off and her breasts are in his hands in seconds while she unzips his neatly pressed khakis. She tosses off Marie Antoinette's bedspread and they're on the very comfy king-sized. "We can make more noise tonight," he says. "I told you, I'm quiet," Kati answers.

With no party downstairs to get back to, they take their time. Satiated, they lie together and talk. "I could get used to this," he tells her. "Yeah," she says, "but don't." "I know, I know," he answers. "But I think about you all the time." "You just have too much time on your hands," Kati laughs. "Go read the tax bill."

"Are you in love?" he asks.

"Oh please. More like we're fuck buddies."

"No. Not me."

"Oh . . . I don't know."

"If you don't know, you're not."

"Yeah. You?"

"Be serious."

"I don't think I could stick around like that. Marriage and kids and all."

"No. Not you. Were you ever?"

"With a boy, back in school maybe. He died."

"Sorry."

"We were so young. You?"

"There's a risk that now -- "

"This? God, no. A risk? You should know, I'm a really bad one." She rolls away. "I assume you're not staying the night," she says. "And I have an early plane."

He leaves. She takes a shower and gets back in bed. She dismisses Good Kati and Bad Kati and decides to stop obsessing on what actual Kati is doing. She sleeps better that way.

Chapter 35

Normally not subject to the inconvenience of introspection, as he drives by the football stadium and on over the Ohio River Brandon Jarrett nonetheless is caught up in thoughts of Kati Case. Is he truly falling in love with her? Could be, although his life experiences don't provide him with much context. He's had more than his share of women, pre- and post-marriage, but love? Hardly.

He does think she's special, she has a definite one-of-a-kindness to her, but that's not love, is it? Even if it's a lot more than he's felt about anything for a while.

It's not fair, he knows, that folks think he married Andrea to get a piece of the Weatherill fortune. Fact is, because the griseofulvin she was taking for toenail fungus rendered her birth control pills ineffective, she wound up pregnant. And at that point, considering that the Weatherill family are long-standing Baptists who frown on abortions, the only option was a wedding he couldn't decline.

So here he is, not so bad off, not at all, with a job that carries prestige and requires not much effort, driving his nice black Lexus -- that he got a special deal on because he's the local Congressman -- to his pleasant house in a Congressional District that every two years sends him back to his Georgetown townhouse and Fairfax mansion with seventy per cent or so of the vote. Sure, there are plenty of mornings when he'd rather not get up and find Andrea, likely hungover, snoring away. But first thing in the morning, doesn't Kati Case roll out of bed red-eyed and bleary, cute pixie hair greasy and standing on end, rush to the bathroom to take a piss, rinse out her mouth, and pull herself together like everyone else.

So why rock the boat? Unlike Kati, though, he doesn't sleep all that well.

Chapter 36

Kati dear,
Thank you so much for taking on my class. They loved you! They want you back, but I told them you're rather tied up right now. After you, I fear I'm just a tired old waste of time to them. At any rate, fortunately I'm quite recovered and back in the world. Text me back when you get a chance
Carter

Carter —
You'll never be a waste of time. Glad you're better. Loved doing it, more fun than in ages. Makes me think I should chuck it all, get my Ph.D, go teach. Seriously. Take care of yourself
Kati

Kati,
Seriously? You'd be bored to death. It's fine for an old goat like me who isn't able to do much else anymore. But at your age, I would have found it terribly stifling. You have so much potential, it's not to waste. Let me know when you're in DC for more than a minute
Carter

Carter —
Being bored can be appealing
Kati

Chapter 37

Lanny Feldbaum is sitting on Randy Carraway's boat in the middle of Lakotah Lake, bundled up in a lime green parka covered in grease stains that was in the back of Carraway's nine-year-old F-150. "It's fucking freezing," he says. "It's 80 in DC and what is it, like 40?" It's also so foggy, or misty, or whatever the fuck it is, that he can't see the shoreline which he assumes is mostly trees, but the asshole seems to know where he's going.

"It's North Dakota, pal," Randy Carraway answers. He's wearing the same flannel shirt and filthy jeans he had on for Lauren Baxter's show, and seems warm enough. His teeth are out. "Might hit 60 by afternoon."

"It's not afternoon. It's 6 in the fucking morning."

"It's when they wake up hungry and they're biting." He stops the boat and casts. "You gonna fish?"

"Why would I fish?"

"You're out on a boat with Lakotah Lake's best fishing guide. And Mayor."

"What would I do with a fucking fish if I caught it?"

"Clean it, take it home, grill it up."

"At the Day's Inn?"

"Got a point there. So what exactly is it that brings you here, Mr. Feldman?"

"Feldbaum."

"Whatever." He reels in, casts again.

"Let's talk some business." He puts up the hood of the parka and jams his hands deeper in the pockets. "You got gloves?"

"Just what I'm wearing. Sorry, pal."

"So anyhow, we can't figure what possibly possessed you to get into this election, but you know there's no chance you can win. But there's ways you can, say, benefit."

"Yeah?"

"What I'm saying is, the President can do things for you, if you do things for him."

"Look pal, get to the point. Oops. Just wait." There's a tug on his line. He plays it and reels it in. A small walleye. He unhooks it and throws it back. "Go on."

"Well tell me first, exactly what you want out of this whole business."

"It's like I said to that woman on the TV and what I keep saying in ads people keep giving me money to put on. I'm a real person, I scrape out a living, I know what it's like. Folks want to hear that. You think I'm expecting to win? Look pal, I took plenty of hits on the coconut when I was playing, but I'm not that crazy."

"Then what?"

"I have a name. I endorse stuff. I'd like to be on TV myself, or at least radio, one of those call-ins. Maybe even one of those between period shows during the hockey games."

"Perfect." Lanny Feldbaum's teeth are chattering, but he forces a smile. "Can do. And some bucks, to tide you over, maybe upgrade the house. Or move out of the old shithole."

"No insults. Remember pal, I'm the Mayor. So what is it you want?"

"Easy stuff. You keep running. People who say they want change or some bullshit like that vote for you instead of Mr. Movie. You have some delegates. And just before the Convention, you say, 'I talked to President Bromwell, and now I know that he's got real people's interests at heart, people like me, so I'm throwing my support to him. Simple, no.'"

"And?"

"We pull strings in the right places, you're on TV and radio, and we put a big load of dough in your campaign account. We've got plenty. Later, you're short maybe, you take some out. You're not running for something anymore, nobody pays attention."

"Like how much are we talking?"

"Six figures. Times something."

Carraway puts down the fishing pole. "This is legal, pal?"

Feldbaum laughs. "This is politics."

"Why not then." He shakes Feldbaum's hand.

"Oh. One more thing," Feldbaum tells him. "These debates they're trying to set up. The President doesn't want to do them. Too busy, you know, running the country. So when he makes an announcement, no debating, you go along. You understand, they're just for show, the Prez has more important things to do, the movie guy just wants an excuse to attack everyone. We'll give you a little script. Got it?"

"Yeah, sure. I don't want no debating either, they just try to put words in my mouth. Hey, pal, you want to borrow my gloves?"

"You bet. And get me back to the damn Day's Inn."

Chapter 38

Agreed, it's not just a one-night stand. So it's twice, big deal. And you know, he's not such a bad guy. And a really good fuck.

Very irresponsible, Kaitlyn. One serious involvement with a married man is bad enough, but this? And he's hardly your type.

I remember, I was maybe 12 when we saw *Wicked*. I thought it was cool, all that girl power. But the cute guy, both girls loved him. Why? I asked. Yeah, he's good looking, but dumb and vacant, and proud of it. Not my type. He was probably good in bed, too.

So is that my type after all? Do I have to have a type? Besides being perfect in everything, do I need to pick perfect guys too? And only one at a time.

Worse yet, Kaitlyn, you don't even seem a bit guilty the second time. That's even worse.

'Bye Lenore.

Chapter 39

Back in Cleveland Heights, Malcolm and Glenda Douglas are having Pho on Coventry Road, a fifteen-minute walk from the little house they started in. The snow is gone, the trees are green, it's nice walking up and down the hills, and they're glad to be home, even if it's only for a day or two.

He doesn't particularly care for the drag of national campaigning, but it hasn't been as bad as he feared. She insists on going along, for the companionship, and to make sure he takes his pills, eats right, and gets enough sleep, and that helps, no doubt about it. It comes naturally to him to talk to people, to walk into a room or a hall, no problem there. Somehow he generates good will, he doesn't know quite how it happens, God's gift he supposes.

Going in, he figures, despite 20-odd years in the Congress, nobody knows him outside of Northeast Ohio. But they do, especially the Black folks. The Carolinas, Atlanta, Alabama through Arkansas, Detroit, St. Louis, he knows why he's on the ticket. Sure, Kati Case talks up all his experience and capabilities, but she's just as up front about demographics. It doesn't bother him, he hasn't been around all this time without figuring out how the game gets played.

It's a challenge to eat here with all the people stopping by to say hello, even to ask for an autograph. That's OK, it's what he's bought into. And it's home.

"You're dripping noodles and soup all over your nice new shirt, Malcolm," Glenda reprimands. "What will all these folks think?"

The shirt's a pale blue striped button-down she bought for him not long ago in Atlanta. He's rarely out of a suit and tie, he says representing the people is an honor and requires dignity, but on home turf he's a bit more casual. He just gives her a shrug. "They'll say I'm a sloppy old fella who's getting harassed by his wife and sits and takes it 'cause she's just as beautiful as the day she agreed to marry him."

"You're an impossible old fella, that's what you are, but I'm glad you did ask. Just in the nick of time, too, before Lanard Jackson beat you to it."

Lanard Jackson, one of his oldest friends, the smartest of their crowd, a tall string bean who played center with Malcolm at Heights High. Not a good enough player to get the power schools interested, he got a scholarship at Case Western, played some Division 3 ball, graduated with a 3.9, went on to the Med School, and wound up an oncologist at Cleveland Clinic. He wishes he could see more of the old guys, some have already passed on, but he's just too busy.

"Lanard never had a chance."

"No. You're right there."

Harry Detwiler walks in and sees them. Retired now, Council President/Mayor for years, he's the one who got Malcolm Douglas into it to begin with. Glenda notices first and waves him over.

Malcolm jumps out of his seat, they hug. "You've got soup all over your shirt, old man," Detwiler says. "Man's running for the highest office in the land and he can't sit down to eat without making a mess."

"Just what I told him," Glenda chimes in.

"Cut out that highest office business. I wouldn't wish that on a Steelers fan. And sit yourself down and see how well you do trying to eat these damn noodles without slopping around," Malcolm says. Harry Detwiler takes him up on it.

"How's it going?" he asks.

"Well enough, I guess."

"I don't know much about this Burnett. What's he like, for real?"

"That's a problem, you know, he doesn't have that high a profile. Frankly, I don't know him all that well myself. Decent guy, by all I can tell, he hasn't made a big splash in the Senate though."

"So how is it -- ?"

"We need someone to take on Bromwell, he's such a disaster. And Wilson Burnett, he sure looks the part, he's capable enough, he raises lots of money."

"How did you get involved, anyway?"

Malcolm Douglas thinks for a moment on how to put it. "Frankly, the whole thing was pretty much engineered by this young Congresswoman from Pennsylvania. Burnett and me both. She's on Ways and Means with me. Very sharp girl."

"Woman!" Glenda interjects. "And pretty too, he always says."

"Cherchez la femme," says Harry Detwiler.

"You could say," Malcolm replies.

Chapter 40

EAR TO THE GROUND
By Roger Newley

With the Primary past the halfway point, this is what The Ear hears.

First, the Democrats. In the Polls composite, it's neck-and-neck:

Bromwell – 40%
Burnett – 39%
Carraway- 9%
Undecided – 12%

Insiders tell the Ear that while Carraway's poll numbers are low, because his strength is concentrated -- in the upper Midwest and in pockets in the rural South -- he stands the possibility of accumulating enough delegates to deadlock the Convention. Asked by The Ear what his plans are if he holds the balance of power for the nomination, Carraway was coy: "I'm running to win, is all I got to say. These polls don't mean squat, watch me when the voting starts."

Our sources are saying that based on past experience, they would expect a significant number of Undecideds to break for Burnett, considering that voters probably have decided what they think of the President, and that Burnett continues to catch up in name recognition. "The Senator is confident that as people get to know him, his support will surge," Kati Case, Representative from Pennsylvania and a leading Burnett supporter, tells The Ear.

Nonetheless, insiders we've spoken to say that even should he pick up a majority of the Undecideds, it's unlikely Burnett can reach the Convention with a delegate majority.

The Ear also hears that President Bromwell will soon announce that he will not participate in the two debates the Democratic National Committee has scheduled for June. A source close to the President, who insists on anonymity, tells The Ear that "because the Presidency requires 18-hour days on his part, there's no time for debates that have proven to be frivolous exercises, so President Bromwell will spend his time doing the job the voters elected him to do."

Asked about the possibility that Bromwell will not debate, Congresswoman Case said: "That would be a President turning his back on the electorate because he's afraid to defend his record. Senator Burnett will be there regardless."

However, when asked his position, Carraway told The Ear that "I haven't given it a second of thought, if they debate I might show up, I might not, you'll find out when it happens, but all that talking's a damn waste of time, politicians should be doing stuff, not running their mouths." So if Carraway also decides not to participate, Senator Burnett could be left with no one to debate with.

As for the Republicans, the picture is clearer. The Polls:

> Villar – 40%
> Marshall – 24%
> Butcher – 19%
> Baggett - 9%
> Undecided – 8%

The inside view, The Ear hears, is that, while three old white men split the traditional vote, focus groups and polling show many Republicans are proving hungry for a new look and have bought into Villar's message of Conservatism With Diversity as the road to the GOP's future viability. The focus groups, we hear, show considerable support for Villar's suggestion to fight climate change and rising water levels with infrastructure improvements, "creating, not destroying jobs," as Villar puts it. Voters are more skeptical of his plan to negotiate with

Cuba to become a 51st state, but are enthusiastic, as one insider put it, "that a Republican can at least have a new idea."

The Ear is also being told to expect an announcement soon from Utah Governor Rolf Baggett, currently running a distant fourth in the polls, that he will suspend his campaign and endorse Villar, a move that could put the Miami Mayor close to the nomination.

That's it for now from The Ear. Have a great Memorial Day holiday.

Chapter 41

Kati Case is at The London World Chronicle offices on NW 18th. With considerable trepidation, she accepts Carter Howell's advice and agrees to be interviewed by Rupert Beveridge. He looks her over a bit too carefully when she arrives. Better than Lauren Baxter, eh Rupert? She's used to it. If she let it bother her every time some guy in this town checked her out, she'd never leave her apartment.

It goes well enough, or at least she hopes so. He's no dope, that's for sure, just like you'd expect from an Oxford prof. A bit flirty, too, for a broken-down old Brit. Well, actually, you could say he's maybe sexy in an over-the-hill kind of way, she can see Lauren's interest. But then, she's at least ten years older than I am. Wilson's eighteen years older than me, that's enough.

All Beveridge does is lob her softball questions. It makes her suspicious, but she can't see what bad he can do with what she has to say.

And she's on her way. Memorial Day weekend in Texas and New Mexico, no time this year for being with Dad at his little house on the Chesapeake. Remember, she's resolved, no whining.

*   *   *

As Rupert Beveridge queries Kati Case, and considers whether she could use a little more meat on her, Marybeth Moran and Roger Newley have managed to get Friday off and are already on the way to Atlantic City in her white Volvo. He finds the car annoying, he hits his head on the door frame whenever he gets in. I'm no giant, he thinks, but the damn car is built for Munchkins. Although if you're Marybeth's size, it's fine.

Driving over the Delaware Memorial Bridge, he's dozing in the passenger seat while she's singing along to *Heart of Gold*, streaming from her phone. "Probably I like the electric stuff more, especially with Crazy Horse, but this is totally classic," she points out. "You know, that's James Taylor and Linda Ronstadt singing the harmony. He did a tour back in the 70's and she was the opening. But I don't think they slept together. I wish I could have seen that."

"Seen them sleep together?" Roger Newley groggily rouses himself to ask.

"No silly, that's gross. Seen the tour."

"Right."

Naturally she's picked the Hard Rock for the weekend, so she can wander around and make believe it's 1970. It's pricy, but she tells him not to worry. It's sunny and in the 70's, they arrive in time to hit the beach. "I burn easily, get it all over," she says as he rubs SPF 100 on her back.

"All over?"

"Don't be a dirty old man," she says and giggles. "Until later."

She sticks her foot in the water, reports back that it's freezing. She looks quite fetching, as promised, in her pink bikini. To say it's on the small size is an understatement. She tells him how much it cost. "But it's like an ounce of material," he says. "Men don't get it," she answers.

She tells him again how much she loves the ocean smell. He notices how it's mixed with the odor of meat frying at a cheesesteak stand up on the Boardwalk, but doesn't argue. Lying together on a very large Washington Nationals towel -- that he ironically got at Beach Day at the Ballpark with Meredith Simmons -- holding hands, he considers he's a pretty lucky guy. Quite the change for Roger Newley. Not given to optimism, he wonders if it's sustainable. And there are still the times, even when she's in bed right up against him, that he wakes up from dreaming of Kati Case. But not so often anymore.

She packs in an unfathomable amount at the buffet. Slabs of roast beef, grilled fish, slice of pizza, sushi, stir-fry. Where does it go? "Metabolism," she says.

Does she want to work it off with a stroll on the Boardwalk? No, she wants to play some blackjack. He's never played, but he can watch. No, it makes her nervous, go find all the memorabilia. She heads to the casino, he walks around looking at things he can report back about, sure she'll need to comment on and check out later. A McCartney guitar ("he was mainly a bass player, but he could play lead, and he played piano, and even drums, amazing"), beads that Janis wore ("so sad about her, makes me want to cry"), one of Leon Russell's top hats ("great with the Cocker tour, not that much into his other stuff, kinda hot in a scary way").

She texts him: "Done. Need to cash in chips. Meet you in the room."

She's sitting on the bed, counting through a wad of cash. "Eight hundred seventy," she says. "Should take care of the weekend pretty much."

"Seriously. You -- ?"

She puts the cash in the room safe. "Don't ever, ever say anything but I can, like, count cards, this boy at MIT taught me, he was hot for me but I wasn't interested, he like washed his hair once a semester at mid-terms. It's not allowed, but if you're not winning, like thousands, they don't pay attention. Especially a girl, they just figure it's a lucky streak and she'll lose it back tomorrow."

"How?"

"Too complicated. You won't get it. It's what I'm good at, another geek thing, like with computers. At work, people are amazed at what I do, they say I'm a wizard, that I learned it at Hogwarts. That I should get a job in Silicon Valley, I could run Google. Should I? What do you think of California. The weather's so nice, but the earthquakes are terrifying, and the fires, and the mudslides, so I'm staying put I guess. And you have a good job."

She's back on the bed. She's in skinny jeans with rips in the knees and an orange summer sweater. He drops down next to her. "I have you," he says, "and wherever we are, that's enough." He thinks he means it. She thinks so too, she shoves him down and dives on top.

Chapter 42

The President of the United States gestures at the TV as a Cardinals hitter completes a home run trot. "I could've hit that pitch. One year they win, and then it's same old, same old. Maybe I should switch to the Sox."

"They suck too," says Lanny Feldbaum. "Stick with the Cubs."

"Everything on track still with Carraway?"

"How many times you gonna ask? He's all set. Thinks he's getting a radio show, maybe TV, and lots of dough. Got reeled in like one of the damn fish he's trying to catch. Asshole."

"Sure you can come through?"

"Come through? What come through? I already told you. You getting senile? Radio, yeah, we'll get someone to put him on, he'll fuck up, and they'll dump him. TV, not likely. Money, fat chance. We'll give him a little from your campaign fund, and that's it. What's he gonna do, sue us 'cause we didn't come through with a bribe we promised. Which we'd deny anyway."

The President looks at a sheet of paper. "You seen this poll?"

"From CNN?"

"Yeah. Says Carraway's getting enough delegates to keep me or Mr. Movie from getting nominated. So he'd better be in the bag."

"For fuck's sake, I was the one told you about it. You getting enough sleep? The delegates, Carraway's sure they'll follow whatever he says. Give it a rest."

"Not sleeping so great, actually. Still worrying about -- oh shit, look at that," the President of the United States yells, "another fucking homer. Can't they get someone who can pitch."

"Wind must be blowing out," Feldbaum replies. "Good, focus yourself on the game."

Chapter 43

Kati Case is back in Philly, begging for money. She hits up old friends and contributors of Paul Winthrop's, makes a run at some Comcast executives, and visits a few big law firms. She spends the night in her childhood bed, meets with the new Phillies owner in the morning, and heads to New York for more of the same.

On the train, she leafs through new polling data. The hope that Bromwell's refusal to debate would hurt him isn't materializing. The internet ad Bloom concocted with their cyber genius, putting Bromwell's head on a chicken body, hasn't done much good. With all the money that's being spent, there isn't much movement. They're still neck-and-neck, Carraway somehow is holding steady, and as it gets later and later, the undecided are staying undecided. And maybe aren't planning to show up?

The Penn Club in New York is on 44th, between Fifth and Sixth, in a 1901 building full of wood and fireplaces, now designated a historical landmark. Usually an uninvolved alum, Kati has never set foot in the place. However, it makes for a likely spot to gather a group of Wall Street Moneybags, several of whom, like Kati, are Wharton grads. Somewhat leery of politics after alumnus Trump, the people in charge decide to give in to the Burnett campaign's request.

In a very business-like charcoal suit with a prim white blouse, nursing a gin and tonic, Kati is virtually the only woman in a cocktail gathering of white men. This must be what it's like to be a Republican, she thinks. Despite her demure look, in half an hour she's already been propositioned, and not too subtly, three times.

Morton Sternberg, chairman of Sternberg, Freud, investment bankers, a plump and balding septuagenarian in a pin-striped three-piece suit is harping on taxes -- which, Kati thinks, is at least better than being hit on. "We're not opposed to progressive taxation, you know, we remain committed to Democratic Party objectives, but you can't suppress growth. We can't turn into England," he mansplains.

"I'd say," she politely answers, "that England's economic issues really can't be explained with reference to its tax policies. If we're going to increase our safety net, and Senator Burnett is committed to that, the money needs to come from somewhere, and it can't be from the poor and middle class."

Nicholas Rockingham, III, head of a very profitable hedge fund, joins in. He seems even younger than Kati and looks rather out of place in faded jeans and a white long-sleeve t-shirt under a blue blazer with gold buttons. The benefits of being so rich you can do whatever you like. Tall, blond, sunken-eyed and not particularly attractive, he has a perpetual sniffle, causing Kati to consider whether too much disposable income is going up his nose.

"Look dear," he says, "I went to Tuck at Dartmouth, we're on the financial front lines and we know about these issues. We understand impacts. What were you, liberal arts, English major?"

"Wharton. Economics." She smiles sweetly. Look dear?

"Yes. So we're confident where Bromwell stands. With you, your man, aren't we taking a risk?"

Kati shakes her head. "It's true Bromwell will do nothing much about anything and maintain the status quo as a result. But I don't see how we can keep on that way. If change costs you a little more, I really think you can afford it. But we recognize, it's your choice, not everyone's willing to go that route. I think, though, you're just going to open yourself up to more radical upheavals down the road."

"I like this girl," says Sternberg. "Spunky. And Senator Burnett comes from business himself, we should be able to trust him. All Mr. Bromwell has done is go from one political office to another, without distinction. So count me in."

Morton Sternberg walks away. Rockingham asks if she'll have dinner with him after. So sorry, but she has to catch a plane. And she takes her spunky self off to a different target.

Chapter 44

Ma Cherie Larrene,
Tu es la plus belle.
Je suis la grosse bombe.
Jesus Leroi

She throws it away again.

Chapter 45

KATI CASE: WIN OR LOSE, THE VICTOR IN THE
PRESIDENTIAL CONTEST
Rupert Beveridge *in Washington for The London World Chronicle*

As the presidential primary enters the home stretch, the focus inevitably
is on the candidates themselves. Thus, observers tend to lose sight of
profound developments occurring in parallel scenes, where the
dramatis personae who perhaps will shape the future are making their
own mark.

One such actor is a young Congresswoman from the birthplace of
American government. Kaitlyn Case -- known to all by "Kati" --
represents Philadelphia in the House of Representatives. The daughter
of former presidential candidate, and now Supreme Court Chief Justice,
Paul Winthrop Case, Ms. Case, now 37, first came to the Congress at
the tender political age of 31 and immediately received notice as a
rising star in the Democratic Party. Progressive and personable,
articulate and charismatic -- and, dare we say, quite pretty -- by her
second term Ms. Case had received appointment to the House's
prestigious Ways and Means committee.

"I guess you could say I grew up on politics," Ms. Case said in our
exclusive interview. "My mother was quite active when my father first
ran for office, and I remember constant dinner-table talk about the
political scene. Unfortunately, she was killed in a car accident my
senior year in college, and, I suppose it would be fair to conclude I
wound up taking over."

The fact is, sources tell us, when Chief Justice Case pursued the
presidency -- and barely missed winning the Democratic nomination --
it was daughter Kati, now established in Congress and only 33, who
was a major force in the campaign. "He wouldn't have come as close as

he did without what she did behind the scenes," according to one source. "She's very smart and very adept."

"I don't know if that's entirely fair," Ms. Case said modestly. "My father's candidacy was based on his merit, which a very large number of voters recognized. And, of course, it's why he now is Chief Justice." But then, what would we expect her to say?

Moreover, the fact is, she's now doing it again, as perhaps the primary engineer of the campaign of Wilson Burnett, the California senator challenging President Daniel Bromwell for the Democratic nomination. This time, however, Ms. Case is more on the front lines, criss-crossing the nation for fund-raising events and public rallies as perhaps the candidate's primary surrogate. "Yes," she said, "I'm definitely out-front more now. It's a function, I suppose, of having been around another four years. And I guess it's easier," she offered with a smile, "when the candidate isn't your father."

Reviews of her performance are brilliant. "Wow," one observer commented, "she has it all. She's a star already and I can't wait to see where she goes from here."

In our interview, Ms. Case downplayed her impact. "A national campaign is so strenuous, the candidates can't do it themselves. Senator Burnett is who voters should be thinking about, he's intelligent and laser-focused on the good of the country. I'm just doing my part."

Ms. Case is married to the New Hampshire governor, Sam Jensen. She says the two are still friendly, but separated, probably permanently. She otherwise refuses to comment on her personal life.

The bottom line as we see it, especially after our get-together, is this: regardless of the winner in this election, keep your eye on Kati Case. She may be your future.

*   *   *

Brandon Jarrett calls. This has become a frequent event, she's given in and answers right away. "Hey sweet thing," he says, "that Beveridge article. If I didn't know you better, I'd wonder what you did for it."

"God, is that what everyone's thinking? All I did was give him an interview, not even a very long one. I had to catch a plane. Who would've thought?"

"Who's he been talking to? You need to put those folks in your contact list."

"Yeah, right. I wonder if he talked to anyone. More likely just made it up. To tell you the truth, it's kind of embarrassing."

"Well, if he talked to me, which of course he didn't, who would, I'd have told him the same thing. So there."

"You can be sweet, you know. It's an unappreciated aspect of your personality."

"Don't know exactly how to take that. Anyway, let me know if you're around."

*   *   *

On a hunch, she calls Carter Howell. "I did put a word in," he admits. Put a word in? "Well actually, I told him to make it good or I'd call some contacts I have at his paper and have him reassigned to Winnipeg. Or the north of Wales. But he was rather taken with you. He has an eye for attractive women, after all."

And where is he getting all his comments from? "Not my business. But I suspect some of it is Ms. Baxter. She's very well connected, you know."

"Lauren? Not possible."

"You'd be surprised."

Chapter 46

"Look," says Yitzhak Kohn, "we can't keep waiting on this."

Chip Chester shakes his head. "We're still working on it."

Kohn drinks so much coffee he keeps a pot going in his office. He fills up his mug. "Working, working, it's bullshit. And time's running out."

"You're over caffeinated, you know that."

"I'm over-tired, over-worked, over-stressed, and over-exasperated. And now I have this." He grabs a report and waves it.

"Which is?"

"Iranians. They're planning for real this time, shooting all sorts of shit at us, bombs, gas, germs. Insects? It's like the fucking Passover plagues. They think because of your fuck-up before, they have a free pass."

"Well we -- "

"Won't do shit. So we have to."

"Meaning?"

"Meaning that we have, maybe a month." He holds up the report again, takes a slug off coffee. "I'm talking with Kidon. If it gets down to a week, we take out the Ayatollah."

Chip Chester gets off his chair. "No."

"Yes. And if it doesn't work, we're in the shelters and the gas masks."

"You'll start a world war."

"Maybe. Maybe not. There's this asset, thinks he-she-it can get in and poison the old bastard. Looks like a seizure, his heart, who knows. But they'll be too distracted to go ahead and attack, and with luck, they'll just bury him and put things off."

"You're clearing this?"

He laughs. "Be serious. How can you possibly think, after, you know. Don't know why I'm even telling you. You need to keep this to yourself. A word, and you're history. We have guys that don't play nice."

"I've heard. You're safe."

Chapter 47

Wilson Burnett starts in Houston, then Phoenix, Vegas and finishes where he started, at L.A. Live. He sleeps at home, where Amber Burnett is feeling much better.

Malcolm Douglas is in Chicago, in the heart of Bromwell country, Milwaukee, Detroit and finally Public Square in downtown Cleveland. He too goes home and will, at Glenda's insistence, vote and spend the next day there before flying back to DC.

Kati Case looks out over a well-attended rally in Washington Square, flies to Pittsburgh, then home to another big one in front of Independence Hall. Bloggers are calling her the third person on the ticket.

She spends the night in her old room, and, at 7:01, she's at the Episcopal church a couple of blocks from home to vote. Local TV stations are alerted, she puts on her biggest smile and waves to her public. Sheryl Sheldon is waiting with the Uber, they go directly to the airport and head

West to join the Candidate for the vote counting.

Guillermo Villar votes and goes home to play with his kids, who have cut school for the big day. The nomination is in the bag. He already has a deal for delegates in exchange for an offer of the vice-presidency with Marshall of Indiana, a veteran senator with reliably conservative views who rarely finds himself burdened with a fresh idea and who has run a distant second in the voting.

The President of the United States takes Air Force One to Chicago first thing in the morning, speaks to a noontime rally that draws a considerably smaller crowd than Malcolm Douglas did hours before, and flies back to the White House. Lanny Feldbaum tells him everything's under control.

Randy Carraway goes out fishing with a very rich guy from Kansas City, a client he guides every year and whom he charges double because he knows he can afford it. He drops the client off at the Hyatt, the best you can do in Lakotah Lake and -- still smelling very much of fish -- goes to cast his ballot.

*　　*　　*

Kati Case is back in the Marriott, in a suite this time, where she, Wilson Burnett, and a few essential staffers will await the results. For the first time in recent memory, there's nothing for her to do. It's a warm and sunny day, L. A. is shimmering in the smog, the surrounding mountains are barely visible. It would be nice, she thinks, to drive out to Santa Monica where the air is cleaner, go down the cliffs to the beach, maybe walk out on the pier. Or even be poolside at Wilson Burnett's house. But by late afternoon, returns from the East will start coming in, so she stays put.

The evening wears on and Burnett's strength throughout the South and Northeast have him holding his own, behind but not by much. Wally Gentry, their pollster, predicts accurately that when the West comes in, he'll pull ahead, by maybe a point nationally. Meanwhile Carraway is getting around seven percent, and accumulating enough delegates to block a first ballot win by either Burnett or the President.

At four in the morning, TruNews produces a delegate count, based on votes, and the exit polls from Alaska and Hawaii:

BURNETT — 1892
BROMWELL — 1851
CARRAWAY — 308
2026 TO NOMINATE

The Candidate goes down to the flag-festooned ballroom to speak to exhausted campaign workers, and to the East and Midwest, which are waking up. It's close, he says, but we appear to have the most delegates and the most votes, and we intend to insist that the Convention honors that. Someone decides that's enough to warrant the release of hundreds of red, white and blue balloons. Wilson Burnett thanks all those who've worked so hard and goes back upstairs, where everyone is preparing to head for the airport to fly back to DC.

If nobody prevails on the first ballot, the so-called super delegates, elected members of Congress and Governors, and a few other higher-ups, get to vote. Many support the status quo above all and will tilt to Bromwell. Malcolm Douglas can work the Congressional Black Caucus. Quite a few will stick with whomever they see as the winner, and let it go at that.

And what of Carraway?

*   *   *

They find out three days later.

Burnett, Douglas, Case, and various underlings, have been trying to reach him. But he neither answers nor returns calls.

On Friday morning, Lanny Feldbaum escorts Randy Carraway from the basement of the Treasury building, through an underground tunnel, and into the White House. Carraway is wearing a black t-shirt with a picture of a yellow perch and a hole at the collar, and red shorts that reach his knees.

Feldbaum tells him to take a shower and lays out a dark suit, white shirt and red tie with black stripes. "What size shoe?" he asks, "you can't wear Tevas." Carraway is not happy about this, but relents when Feldbaum insists it's part of the deal.

The President of the United States has lunch with the two of them. They silently eat cheddar burgers. Carraway thinks they're not as tasty as Feldbaum led him to believe. "Now you can say you've met with the President," Feldbaum points out, "because we're all about honesty."

Feldbaum hands Carraway a typed-up set of notes, and spends much of the afternoon rehearsing. At around five, he instructs Carraway to put his teeth in, has a staffer skilled in hair care rubber-band his newly shampooed mop into a pony tail, helps him tie his tie, and, with Feldbaum on board, has him driven to TruNews, where at six he will once again talk with Lauren Baxter.

"Well hello again," she greets him, surprised at his slick new look. She's wearing a flowery pink blouse, open several buttons down where her microphone gets clipped on.

"Hello to you, lady," he says, trying to see if any boob is visible.

She hasn't been told why he's asked to come on, but since the call came from the White House, she has a pretty good idea.

Kati Case is sitting on her sofa with Wilson Burnett. "Oh shit," she says when Carraway appears.

"So Mr. Carraway, congratulations on your very colorful campaign."

"What's that supposed to mean, lady?"

Lanny Feldbaum holds his breath. Lauren Baxter ignores him. "What do you have to tell us today?" she asks.

He lays his notes out, pauses while he looks them over another time. "Well it's like this. I've had a sit down with Bromwell, the President you know, and he's a good guy. He understands a real guy like me." He looks down again, decides he's not going to go through all the crap Feldbaum's written. "So I'm telling my delegates to vote for him."

"We're fucked," says Kati Case.

"That's it?" says Lauren Baxter. "No other rationale?"

"No other what?"

"Reason."

"You heard me."

"And your delegates, you expect them to . . . do what you say?"

"Lady," says Carraway, thumping his fist on the table, "they'll do whatever I tell them."

Lauren Baxter looks straight at the camera and rolls her very blue eyes. "Can I ask you one more thing?"

"Sure. It's your show."

"What exactly are you getting paid for this?"

"I can't believe she asked that," says Kati Case.

Lanny Feldbaum gestures wildly from off camera for Carraway to get out of there. He obediently picks up his notes and walks off.

"But we are fucked," says Kati.

Wilson Burnett sighs and turns to her. "Well, I guess. But, you know, you do what you can, and then. . . . And . . . I love you, you know."

What timing, she thinks. "Love you too," she says.

Chapter 48

Now what, Kaitlyn? Nice mess.

You again? Like you would've somehow done it better. Actually, Dad would've won four years ago, right? Too bad you left a little girl to do a grown-up job.

And Wilson? Yes, Kaitlyn, what about your Wilson?

Yeah, I know what I told him, but people say all sorts of things. Maybe we'll just keep it up this way, Wilson, Amber and Kati. Lucky Amber, she gets to stay in LA. Lucky Kati, she gets . . . what? And it's Kati. K-A-T-I. Kati.

Chapter 49

Wilson Burnett is golfing with Malcolm Douglas and Walt Morelli, the chairman of the DNC and the former Governor of Massachusetts, who somehow managed to lose his bid for a second term. Why, Kati Case wonders, do we put some nonentity who can't even manage to win in Massachusetts in charge of the party? And he's the guy who picked out Bromwell four years ago.

Kati isn't invited to golf with the boys. She doesn't play anyway. She played basketball in high school, mostly as a three-point shooting guard ("Pass it sometimes, Case"). A decent tennis player too, second singles, but she hasn't played in a while. I should get back into it now that I'll have more time, she thinks. And I have to start running again.

Left at home, she's on the web investigating degree programs and the possibility of taking classes part-time, maybe in January. The Washington schools would be logistically simpler, but really, she'd rather be back at Penn. She could be in Philadelphia a couple of days a week, sleep in her old bed, take classes, and do constituent service -- sit in the office she keeps in her district and listen to people complain in person. The school for sure would work something out for her, not only is she somewhat famous, she had a 3.8 GPA as an undergrad and she's always aced standardized tests. For God's sake, they took all those Trumps. She thinks about taking back one of the Eagles season tickets her cousin's been using since her part of the family decamped for DC. And later, settling down in a nice college town, maybe Palo Alto, or Ann Arbor, but what she really feels right now is a deep longing to go home.

*　　*　　*

Walking between the seventh green and the eighth tee, Walt Morelli raises the prospect of Wilson Burnett's releasing his delegates and supporting Bromwell's nomination by acclimation. "Fuck that,"

Malcolm Douglas, not normally given to cuss words, spits back.
Burnett himself is silent.

"You can have a prime-time speech slot," Morelli offers. "You
too Malcolm." "Fuck that, too," he replies. "Far as I'm concerned, it's
going to be a roll call, and we'll see how the idiot's delegates vote."

"Wilson?"

"Let's just play golf," he says.

Patently annoyed, Malcolm Douglas has honors and takes it out
on his Titleist which he slams 300 or so yards into the edge of the
rough. "Man, you're long off the tee," Morelli comments.

"I picture a face on the ball and let it go," Malcolm answers. He
doesn't say what face.

*   *   *

Brandon Jarrett calls Kati to commiserate. He's not pushing
anything, giving her space, he says. He's actually pretty decent all in
all, too bad he's not a Democrat. Then I could not only fuck him I
could talk him into running for President in four years? She decides to
go to the pool to swim some laps.

She showers off the chlorine. Blow drying her hair, she looks at
herself and thinks she sees lines on her face. And a couple of gray
spots. Maybe I should grow my hair out, it hasn't been long since 10th
grade. Amber says things get way simpler when you get older and
people don't notice you so much.

Carter Howell calls. "You knew when you got into it there'd be
ups and downs. It's the game. You move on."

"Or move out," she says.

"Back to that, are we? This is hardly the time for precipitous
conclusions on the future. Forget this recent adversity, it's only good
for you, you know, in the long run. You've taken major steps to build a
national profile."

"So?"

"Why you could run yourself next time. JFK was only 43 when
he was elected."

"I know you want to make me feel better," she answers, "but that's the last place I want to be going."

She stares out the window at the neatly mowed lawn and carefully trimmed trees her condo dues pay for. She goes to the fridge, pours a glass of lemon-flavored seltzer, and has some hummus and chips and a lo-fat yogurt.

Lauren Baxter calls. How does she have my cell number? Beveridge probably.

"I'm sorry about what happened," she starts out. "I just want to let you know that I'm not the one who decided to have that dickhead make his big announcement on my time. At least they cleaned him up. We needed to spray air freshener all over the place when he was on before."

"I appreciate the call," Kati says. "Really. You didn't exactly hide what you were thinking, when you asked that last question."

"Wouldn't we like to know the answer. Well anyway, we should get together some time. Or you could come on the program if you'd like."

"I'm thinking of staying out of sight for now, but thanks. Maybe drinks after the convention, when things calm down."

That was a surprise. A person I maybe misjudged?

Wilson Burnett comes back. He doesn't seem all that distressed over how things have worked out. Maybe he's relieved. He tells her about Morelli, and Malcolm's reaction. "Good for him," she says. "Morelli's such a schmuck."

They go out for Italian to an unpretentious place on Lee Highway. No tablecloths. The walls have pictures of the Old Country, where the new owner, a second-generation Vietnamese, has surely never been. She has angel hair with basil, garlic and tomatoes; he has linguine with mussels and clams. They split a carafe of the house red.

The Convention's in Boston, thanks to Morelli. She says she's never been to Fenway, she needs to figure out who to call for tickets. He'd like to skip it, but he needs to go for at least a day or two. McWillis is heading home to Pine Bluff, he wonders who Bromwell's picking for Vice. Not me, she says. He laughs. Afterwards, she's going to the Bay with the Chief Justice. He's heading home. He's like a time share, she thinks, I have my weeks, Amber has hers. She keeps that to herself.

Back home, they watch a cop show, go to bed, make calm love, and fall asleep.

Chapter 50

On a stifling July morning, Roger Newley is waiting for Kati Case under an umbrella outside the Peet's Coffee by the White House. With so much less to do, she's only a few minutes late. The Republican Convention is next week, the Democrats the week after, he's hoping for some inside dope for The Ear.

He has an iced mocha latte; she has a double espresso, apparently oblivious to the temperature. He still finds her dazzling, but he's less obsessed. He tells her about his new girlfriend. Kati tells him she sounds like a keeper. She hopes so. He can use it.

Nothing's been announced, but Kati confirms that everyone knows Marshall will be Villar's running mate. What she's hearing is that Bromwell's planning on Ned Yullin, the mayor of Buffalo, to replace McWillis. Why, she has no idea. Not a sure thing yet, but worth going with, she tells him.

He asks about rumors that Burnett and Douglas are refusing to endorse Bromwell and are considering a third-party run. She laughs and shakes her head. "But write it up," she says, "make the fuckers squirm a little. He's not endorsing until after the Convention, maybe a while after, so for a while you'll look like a genius. And let them keep worrying he's thinking third party."

She leaks an internal poll to him, that's been leaked to her and who knows who else, that shows Villar leading Bromwell by six points. The same poll has Burnett up two. "At this point, I could care less," she adds. "But don't write that."

He looks over his shoulder as she walks away. Out of my league, I'm lucky I found Marybeth. He heads to his crummy office to work on the column.

But he's still thinking about Kati Case when Marybeth calls. She sounds hyped up, even for her. "You have to come over tonight. I've got something serious to tell you. Really serious. Really big."

"About?" he asks.

"No. I can't talk over the phone. It's like so secret, I can only say it in person, and I have to show you something, you'll be amazed, it's huge, and we have to stay in, I'll make pasta or something, I have wine so you don't have to bother, but like 6:30 or so would be good. OK?"

"OK," he says. Fine with him.

Roger Newley is a prompt person -- why not he tells people, I have the time. He expects water to be boiling and sauce to be heating, but there's no sign she's thinking about dinner, except for the bottle of Zinfandel that she's opened and started on. Some papers are spread out on her coffee table next to the wine. She kisses him and goes to the sofa.

She points at the coffee table. "You won't believe what that is, neither can I, I didn't have much to do today, so I was fooling around, I do that sometimes, I try to see what kind of stuff I can find, I'm like hacking our own stuff, if anyone asks I can say I'm doing a security check, and hardly anyone can follow what I'm up to anyway, and then -- " She hands him the papers. "I was going to forward it to myself, but I thought, maybe someone'll trace that, so I printed it out."

Roger Newley picks it up. He sees a lot of numbers he doesn't understand. One is ridiculously large: IRR 84,210,000,734.00. "I don't get it," he says. "IRR?"

"I looked all this up, IRR is the currency code for Iranian Rials, it's their money, that number, it's like 84 billion and something, it's like two million U.S. dollars. And see this." She points to letters DBS. "It's a bank in Singapore. And see this. It's an account number. And guess who's account?"

"Not mine, for sure." He picks up the wine from the coffee table and pours himself a glass.

"Daniel P. Bromwell."

"No."

"Yes."

"And how -- ?"

"I have ways. I go all Hermione, and someone really fucked up. This should have been encrypted so nobody could get it, I could've done it, but obviously they weren't asking me, I don't know who did it, but they don't know what they're doing, I mean they know something, it was pretty well buried, but not enough, at least not enough when I got after it."

Roger Newley looks more closely. "This date. It's the transfer?"

"I guess. I mean, what else can it be, they don't just put, like, random dates on bank records, so that's what I figure, yeah."

He takes out his phone, does a fast google search. "It's the week before we went into Iran and the Revolutionary Guard was waiting."

"Correct. I checked that right away. Amazing, huh? And there's something else." She hands him another piece of paper. A copy of what looks like an email:

To: Bozo
From: G
Subject: Take care of General

"What's this?"

"Check your calendar. When were you supposed to meet with that guy who got murdered?"

He looks. "Oh my God. Like two days after this."

"That's what I thought, and he wanted to talk to you, and it couldn't be on the phone, or in your office or anything, and he sounded like he thought it was something huge, and I don't think we can prove anything, not from just this, but when you think about it, you know, this other stuff, the money and all, Bromwell, and he was at the Pentagon, right, I think he knew what happened and he was going to tell you, and someone offed him. That's what I think." She catches her breath, finishes the Zinfandel in her glass and fills it up again. He does the same. "So you need to get this in the paper ASAP. Not the General, we don't have enough, and it's a sideshow, it's the money from Iran and all. And Bromwell."

Roger Newley shakes his head. "I can't," he tells her.

"You have to."

"No. I'm your boyfriend. It wouldn't take long for whoever to figure out where it came from. Like the reason you didn't forward it to yourself. Look at what happened to Hurley. So -- "

"Roger Newley, you have to, we're talking earthshaking news, it's the most huge thing ever, it's the biggest story of your life."

He drinks some more wine, puts his arm around her. "No," he says, "you're the biggest story of my life." He calls Kati Case.

*   *   *

Kati Case isn't excited about driving up the Baltimore-Washington Parkway to Roger Newley's girlfriend's apartment at eight at night to discuss something he couldn't even mention on the phone, but he sounds really serious. She tells Wilson Burnett where she's off to and why and drives off with the top down on her cute red Miata.

She gets it right away. Roger and Marybeth are on the sofa. Marybeth thinks Kati is nice looking, for her age. The wine bottle is empty by now. Kati is pacing around. "Jeez," she says, "I thought he was an idiot. But this is fucking treason. And then, poor Hurley. You're right, though, you can't be the one to write it." She nods at Marybeth.

"So what do we do?" Marybeth asks.

Kati calls Rupert Beveridge.

*   *   *

Rupert Beveridge and Lauren Baxter are eating popcorn and watching Rear Window for at least the third time. Her son is at his Dad's. Kati Case tells him it's the biggest story he can imagine, with luck it can be his rehabilitation. Lauren can come too.

They're all in Marybeth Moran's living room. She opens the evening's third bottle of wine.

"Well," Beveridge concludes, "since I've been here, I've certainly seen a lot. But this. Incomprehensible, but there it is."

"I can't wait 'till we get it on air," Lauren Baxter says. "You should be planning on an appearance, Kati, looks like you're going to be back campaigning. And you did this? All by yourself?" she asks Marybeth.

By this point, even Marybeth is pretty well out of words. She just shrugs.

"I think, Kati says, "it might be smart to get your ass to London before it goes public. If what we think about Hurley -- "

No one disagrees.

Chapter 51

Monday 7 a.m.

Looking groggy, the President of the United States stumbles into the Oval Office. The TV is on, Lanny Feldbaum is walking up and down. "Finally," he says, voice rising, "what the fuck's this shit." He points at the screen.

"What?" the President asks. "The Republican Convention's starting tonight? Who cares?"

"Just listen," Feldbaum tells him.

The TruNews morning anchors, a blonde woman and a man with a neat beard, are talking about a report from London. Bribe. Iran. President Bromwell. Treason? The President looks astonished.

"Well?" asks Lanny Feldbaum.

The President of the United States pulls himself together. He may not think all that quickly, but he's been a politician long enough to talk fast. "This is from some Englishman? Sitting his ass in London. It's all bullshit. It's a frame-up. It's a hoax. It's fake news. It's Burnett and his friends. It's the Iranians setting me up. It's the Russians. It's bots. They can't prove anything, what've they got, some piece of paper. Do something about it."

"You want to talk to the press?"

"Fuck, no. Get something out. Like I just said. Deny everything."

"Got it," says Feldbaum, and walks out. He wonders.

Monday 7:18 a.m.

Wilson Burnett, in a white golf shirt and light tan slacks, is up early to try to get nine holes in before it gets too hot. "You have to see this," says Kati Case, who has the TV on. For days she's managed to keep to herself what she knows -- until Beveridge can make it to London and get the story out.

"God almighty," he exclaims, "it can't be real."

"I think it is," she says.

"What do we do?"

"A fast presser. Noon, across from the White House. I like the optic. Short statement, no questions. I'll set it up, get something drafted. Go keep your golf date."

"Right."

Monday 9:12 a.m.

The F.B.I., accompanied by Deputy Attorney General Braithwaite, serve a search warrant, approved by the Attorney General himself, at the White House, seize various pieces of computer equipment, and question the tech specialists about what they might know. No one has any idea. It's July, remember, so several workers are on vacation. Marybeth Moran, for example, is home in Erie, Pennsylvania, introducing her boyfriend, who she's very serious about, to her parents.

Monday 9:53 a.m.

The White House issues a statement that the report circulating is a baseless story from overseas, which is a frame-up, fake news, a hoax, concocted by elements in the Democratic Party opposed to the President and disgruntled by his pending nomination, a set-up by Iranians, conceived by Russians, and spread by bots. And that the Attorney General's resignation has been accepted.

Monday 10:06 a.m.

Just past five in the afternoon in Tel Aviv, Chip Chester is wishing he was done for the day, when he gets the call he's been expecting from Yitzhak Kohn demanding his presence.

Kohn has his feet up on his desk and smiles when Chester walks in. "Your guys couldn't get bupkis and some old fart in London figures it all out? And your great President, this is what we get. For crying out loud, if he wanted a pay-off, we could've done a lot better."

"A mystery to me," Chip Chester says.

"For what it's worth, it maybe just saved the Ayatollah. We're all set to go. Another couple of days and he's a dead man. But we think the fucking Iranians are going to hold off now, with this stuff out there."

Monday Noon

Wilson Burnett, still in his golfing outfit, addresses the press, Malcom Douglas and Kati Case standing behind him, White House in the background. The temperature is 94, with the Capital's normal swampy humidity. He is, as always, measured and composed, a calming influence for a disturbed national psyche.

"This is a dark day for our country," he says. "An unfathomable accusation, apparently well founded, that the President has engaged in treasonous conduct in the pay of a foreign enemy. It truly was our Founding Fathers worst fear. Of course, the President is entitled to defend himself -- if he possibly can -- but we cannot allow this cloud to long remain over us.

"Although some will say this is not the time for political considerations, we cannot ignore that a week hence, the Convention of our party will begin, and consideration of whether the President can conceivably be nominated will be foremost. In this regard, I have no choice but to point out that in the recent primary voting, I received more votes and won more delegates than the President. Under the present unprecedented circumstances, I therefore intend to demand that the Democratic National Committee amend its rules to free delegates to vote their conscience, and I will go to the Convention and urge each and every delegate to support my nomination.

"Thank you all and pray for our Republic."

Assembled reporters shout questions. "Not now," he smiles and walks off. "Nice job," says Malcolm Douglas. "Nice little statement," he says to Kati Case. "I thought so," she replies.

Monday 3 p.m.

The President of the United States has disappeared into his private quarters. Lanny Feldbaum hasn't seen him since early morning. The President hasn't even joined him for the Cubs game. The press is clamoring for an appearance. Feldbaum tells the White House press secretary to tell them the President is tied up with important business of state.

Monday 4 p.m.

Randy Carraway comes home, sticks four fish in the freezer, and to his surprise finds his girlfriend and 13-year-old son from a previous woman watching the news in the living room. He absorbs what's happening. "That really sucks," he says. "Now those dicks'll never pay up."

Monday 5 p.m.

The F.B.I.'s tech specialists have made no progress in figuring out how to get to the data uncovered in the Beveridge story.

Kati Case arrives at TruNews for her appearance on the Lauren Baxter show, an hour ahead of time at the host's request.

Lauren Baxter is having her hair done. A pitcher of Bloody Mary's is sitting on a nearby table. Kati points at it and laughs.

"You don't think I can do this five nights a week without some help?" she tells Kati. "Sit down, it's not all for me."

Kati pours one. "To crooked politicians," she says.

"I liked the Senator's little speech before," Lauren says, joining Kati's toast. "Just the right pitch. You wrote it, right?"

"Now why would you say that?"

"First of all, I'm supposed to know everything. Second, everyone knows."

"No comment," Kati grins.

"Your hair's fine, I'd love to go short, but they won't let me. But you need a little makeup."

"Funny. I was thinking of growing it out. And I really don't . . . makeup. Kind of not my thing."

"It's the lights. You need something. Try to make sure she's not that much prettier than me," she says to the woman finishing her hair.

Lauren Baxter tells Kati she's had her come in early so they can get to know each other. They discuss the election; Lauren talks about having a child which she never thought she'd want to do, and Kati says she's still not interested in; and then they reminisce about men. They agree to not get into current partners. They compare notes on some shared involvements from the past, and offer thoughts on others they've known. Lauren Baxter, Kati notes, has a far more extensive roster, but then again, she's got a ten-year or so head start. Lauren's include Brandon Jarrett, she gives him an A in bed, a C otherwise. Kati holds her tongue.

"I have a question," Kati says. "You started out as an Orange County Republican. How did you wind up here?"

"You know," Lauren Baxter answers, "at some point you realize that all the politics is mostly horseshit, and you start making decisions on who you like as people. That's all." She pauses. "And something else . . . I can't really talk about."

With much of the Bloody Mary pitcher under their belts, they go on the air. Kati is still in the rose pastel blouse she's had on all day and black pants. Lauren is wearing a yellow pull-over on top, ordinary jeans down below, hidden from the camera by her desk.

Lauren doesn't kid around. "Joining me today is my friend Representative Kati Case, a major force in the presidential campaign of Senator Wilson H. Burnett. Representative Case is here because today of all times we need some fresh air and we need to hear from someone who shows you can be in politics and still keep your integrity. Because today we've found out that our President is a slimy, sleazy, crooked, dishonest, traitor who'd sell out his country for profit." She stops. "Oops." She taps her earpiece. "They're telling me I have to say 'alleged' according to the lawyers. So, today we've found out that our alleged President is an alleged slimy, alleged sleazy, alleged crooked, alleged dishonest, alleged traitor, who'd allegedly sell out his country for alleged profit. OK? Got that? Tell us, Kati, what's it all mean."

"So," Kati says, "you've done a nice job making the point, haven't you. But what we have to remember is that we need to go forward. Together. What we've found out today is horrible, but we can get past it. We will, I'm sure we will."

"She's more diplomatic than I am," Lauren says with a big grin. "That's why she's still in politics and I'm not. But tell me Kati, what's this mean for the campaign. Can the Democrats survive this?"

Another softball. "Sure," Kati answers. "Senator Burnett's integrity has never been questioned. He's smart, honest, he's exactly what we need now. And, you know, he had the most votes and delegates. So with him as our nominee, I'm absolutely confident we'll win."

"And Bromwell, would you have him prosecuted?"

"Let's leave that to the lawyers. And maybe not today."

Today can't be soon enough for Lauren Baxter. She trots out a white-collar criminal lawyer down from New York, a former U.S. attorney, and a professor from Georgetown. At the break, she tells Kati she's moving to other topics so she can take off. But they should get together after the Convention. Definitely Kati tells her. Is this woman, she thinks, who I thought I couldn't stand, going to be a best friend?

Monday 9 p.m.

In Atlanta, Guillermo Villar, the presumptive nominee, makes an unprecedented first night appearance at the Republican Convention to say that each and every member of the Democratic Party is responsible for the President's corruption.

Tuesday 8 a.m.

Anonymous sources report that the F.B.I has made no progress in confirming the information reported in yesterday's London World Chronicle article, although they have no reason to disbelieve it.

Tuesday 9 a.m.

The White House issues a brief statement that the F.B.I's inability to find the supposed information on the computers they've illegally seized proves the accusations are a hoax. Lanny Feldbaum prepares the release. He hasn't seen the President since yesterday morning.

Tuesday 11:30 a.m.

The F.B.I receives a message from a burner phone, traceable by cellular triangulation to Cleveland, that provides a detailed road map for finding the data set out in The London World Chronicle article.

Tuesday noon.

A small and attractive young woman with red hair and pretty green eyes strolls through the Flats. She stops to look down at the once-maligned Cuyahoga, the centerpiece of a now trendy neighborhood, and drops a small object into the river where it quickly sinks. She walks away, stops in a neat little bistro where she finishes every bite of a SuperMax Burger with fries, goes to her white Volvo with Maryland plates, and drives off east on I-90 toward Pennsylvania.

Tuesday 5 p.m.

The F.B.I. announces, in time for the evening news, that it has been able to confirm information contained in recent news reports concerning the deposit of Iranian funds into the account of Daniel P. Bromwell. It will have no comment on further steps, pending consultation with the Acting Attorney General.

Tuesday 5:09 p.m.

Lanny Feldbaum phones Vince Lamont, Esquire, in Chicago. Told by Mr. Lamont's personal assistant that he has not yet returned from court, Feldbaum leaves a message: "Get to DC ASAP."

Wednesday 2 a.m.

The President of the United States, dressed in a full burqa, slips out of the White House to a waiting Ford Expedition, which, scrupulously observing the speed limit, drives him to Dulles International, where he boards a plane parked at a remote spot on the airfield and departs. He leaves behind a wife, dog, hand-written note, and Lanny Feldbaum.

Wednesday 6:13 a.m.

Lanny Feldbaum walks into the Oval Office. On the Resolute Desk is a sheet from a legal pad:

I resign.

Daniel P. Bromwell

Wednesday 7:38 a.m.

Lanny Feldbaum is placed under arrest by the F.B.I. He says nothing. Shortly thereafter, his attorney tells reporters that Mr. Feldbaum has no knowledge whatsoever of President Bromwell's evil dealings and is completely innocent.

Wednesday 10:01 a.m.

Chief Justice Paul Winthrop Case hurries to the White House where he swears in Clement McWillis as President of the United States.

Wednesday 1p.m.

President McWillis meets with the Chief Justice's daughter, Wilson Burnett, and Malcolm Douglas in the Cabinet Room, where the Cabinet itself will assemble shortly. Several portraits of Lincoln, hung at the direction of the former First Lady, look down.

McWillis sits at the head of the table, in front of the ornate fireplace. Busts of Washington, over his right shoulder, and Franklin, over the left, observe. Senator Burnett and Representative Douglas sit to his right hand, Representative Case to his left.

"Now y'all surely know why you're here, boys and girl. Old Clem is in sore need of some help, and pronto. I've been around here for almost four years and I haven't done squat exceptin' for shakin' hands with folks who aren't important enough for anyone else to, and I don't plan on startin' now."

Did Washington just roll his eyes? Old Ben suppresses a chuckle.

"Now just be calm, Mr. President," Malcolm Douglas starts out.

"Make it Clem," McWillis interrupts.

"Right. Clem. Anyway," Douglas resumes, "listen to your Cabinet. They aren't going anywhere. Mostly they're OK. You just need to get through six months."

"But what if I have to decide something? I'm assuming it's you folks gonna be runnin' and I sure don't want to screw you up."

"Just call me. Or Malcolm, or Kati," Wilson Burnett says. "If need be, we'll fly back to Washington."

"Well if it's a face-to-face, I'd sure prefer this youngun' here," he says, pointing at Kati. "Seein' her's good for an old man's morale." He pauses. "Just kiddin' you know."

"Probably not," Kati says, but she does manage a smile. "But I'll take it as a compliment."

"Well you should. I'm too far gone for that politically correct bullshit when it comes to a pretty young woman. Anyway, I suppose now I need to make a speech next week."

"Afraid so," says the Senator. "But Kati will write you something."

"That makes three," she says.

"I'll do my own," says Malcolm Douglas.

"Not you. Me. Considering everything, I want a prime-time slot Monday or Tuesday." An idea Lauren Baxter pushed her to pursue when they talked earlier.

"I like that, says," says Malcolm. "Glenda and I were just talking about it."

"Oh. Why not?" says Wilson Burnett. It hadn't occured to him? Men. Even the good ones can be so oblivious, she can hear Lauren saying.

"Make it short," says McWillis. "I can't stay standing up that long, and I've got some emphysema. All those damn cigarettes, it's a miracle I'm alive. But who knew? Actually, everyone, we smoked 'em anyway."

"Got it," Kati says.

He ushers them out. Soon the Cabinet will arrive. What was it Bromwell supposedly said his first day, what the fuck am I doing here. Ain't it the truth.

Wednesday 4:29 p.m.

The former President of the United States lands at Tehran Iman Khomeini International Airport. Wearing a red polo shirt, pale blue slacks, and white loafers, he hastily transfers to another plane and immediately leaves.

Wednesday 4:45 p.m.

On a partly cloudy July day, Roger Newley and Marybeth Moran sit on a towel on the beach at Presque Isle State Park in Erie, Pennsylvania. The lake is calm, you could even say it's sort of blue, the water temperature in the mid-70's. Looking fetching in her pink bikini, which her mother believes is on the skimpy side, Marybeth has been swimming and even managed to get her boyfriend in. She says they need to start heading home, her folks like dinner early.

"I have a question," he says.

"Yes?"

He takes a deep breath. "Will you marry me?"

"Of course," she says and hugs him.

"The ring's on hold in Kay's on U.S. 1 in downtown Laurel. I was afraid, you know, you wouldn't say yes."

"That," she answers, "is one of the craziest things you've ever said."

Wednesday 10:12 p.m.

Daniel Bromwell, private citizen, lands at Velana International Airport in the Maldives, where the local time is just after nine Thursday morning. The Maldives are known for, among other things, being strictly Muslim, prohibiting dogs (cats OK), being the repository of apparent wreckage from the ill-fated and mysteriously disappeared Malaysian Airlines flight 370, and having no extradition treaty with the United States. English, he has been told, is widely spoken. Mr. Bromwell is whisked off to a house purchased in his name near the ocean -- which, he has been told, is safe from shark attacks -- where he expects to quietly reside.

Chapter 52

"The government of the Islamic republic of Iran knows nothing about statements that money has been paid to the American President. Or the former American President as we are now informed."

"But isn't there proof that Iranian funds, the equivalent of approximately 2 million United States dollars, were placed in the President's, former President's, account?"

"As I said, we know nothing of this. Perhaps a wealthy and patriotic Iranian provided these funds to him in the hope that it would lessen the Satanic practices of the United States. If so, it appears not to have succeeded in its goal. However, we know nothing of this, as I said."

"What of the timing? Just before an ill-conceived military action by the United States that Iran easily repelled as if it had warning?"

"The bravery of our soldiers speaks for itself."

"Do you have knowledge of the former American President's whereabouts?"

"How should we know such a thing? Ask the Americans."

"So you're saying the timing, it's all a coincidence?"

"Thank you for your time. Good day."

*　　*　　*

Daniel Bromwell can see the water from his window through the palms. After checking Google Maps on the new Galaxy phone he's been provided with, he decides it's probably the Indian Ocean. It sure isn't Lake Michigan. Both air and water temperature are in the mid-80's, with a nice breeze. He'd like to stroll the beach, perhaps take a swim in the supposedly shark-free water, but he's been told it would be wisest to lay low for a time. And he does have a pool.

His housekeeper, who seems to come with the property, is a rotund woman of a certain age who speaks limited English. She serves him his breakfast, a mixture of rice, local fish -- he would hope so, it's the middle of a damn ocean -- bits of coconut, and unidentifiable sauces and condiments. He picks at it. Other meals so far are similar. Better get used to it.

This is, of course, not the way things were supposed to work out. Someone really fucked up. He's hopeful his wife can get along, he wonders if all his pensions are being revoked. He misses the dog. They will, however, shortly get him a cat. He'd like to talk things over with Feldbaum. It seems unlikely there's a way to get the Cubs games. But, you deal the hand you get, they say. That doesn't sound right. Whatever.

*　*　*

Walt Morelli wants advice before he convenes anyone else on the DNC. He meets with Charles Gray, very well-connected Washington counsel with Democratic leanings, senior partner of McCormack and Gray. McCormack is long dead, but his presence remains via his portrait hung in the conference room. A rather grumpy looking fellow, with a shock of white hair and silver spectacles, Marybeth Moran would wonder if he's going to offer his opinion like the old headmasters on the walls at Hogwarts. Charles Gray is much cheerier, slim and sleek with neatly coiffed black hair (dyed? a rug?) in a tan suit that befits the District's summer swelter, blue shirt, and red power tie. Morelli by contrast is a nondescript balding fellow of medium height and medium build with a narrow mustache that, Lauren Baxter once said, looks like there's a centipede crawling across his upper lip.

Sitting in are a law professor flown down from Harvard, another constitutional expert from Georgetown, and an old friend of Gray's, Carter Howell.

"Is there any rule about this?" Morelli asks.

The professors indulge in an abstruse discussion of the lack of specific Constitutional provisions, extrapolations from extant Constitutional language, and what Madison and Hamilton would do.

"Perhaps sing?" Gray suggests. "Carter?"

"I'm not sure precisely why, Charles, I'm even here, in the midst of all this legal expertise."

"Common sense, I'd say."

"Accepted. Well, if I understand the situation correctly, and of course I may not, there's no real legal structure to speak of. Historically, one thing of which we can be certain is at the time the Republic was founded, there were no political parties at all, and certainly no primary contests. So it appears, Mr. Morelli, you're free to proceed."

"Meaning?" Morelli asks.

"Meaning," says Carter Howell, "you should, as expeditiously as possible, figure out an efficient way to modify whatever rules the DNC is operating under to get Burnett nominated so you can put Bromwell and this Carraway buffoon in the rear-view mirror."

"Concur," says Charles Gray. "Are we done? I have clients waiting."

Morelli catches a cab back to his office near the Capitol and tells his secretary to set up a conference call with the rest of the DNC executives. He leafs through his messages. The one from Kati Case is suddenly of high priority: I want a speaking slot, prime time, Monday or Tuesday; Red Sox tickets for whichever night I'm not speaking. Morelli reaches for his bottle of acetaminophen.

*　　*　　*

Back in Miami, Guillermo Villar holds his first press conference as the Republican nominee. This one is on dry land. He starts with the thought that every person who is, or was, a Democrat, or ever voted for one, is in some way responsible for what he describes as the greatest disgrace and treason, not only for the United States, but in the history of mankind. Perhaps a bit hyperbolic, someone suggests. Not at all, he says, you support corruption when you condone corruption. And you condone corruption when you support corruption. The answer to every question finds it way back to "Benedict Arnold Bromwell." Or "Judas Bromwell."

"Furthermore," he adds, "the traitor now has disappeared and none of his Democratic collaborators can find him. So I promise this. When I am President, on my first day in office I will set out to find Judas Bromwell. If I have to do it myself, if I have to search the world, I will bring him to justice."

"You're personally going to go after him?" an incredulous L.A. Times reporter asks.

"Why not. I come from a band of citizens that won't back down. If we need the Cisco Kid, I'll be the Cisco Kid."

"Wasn't he Mexican?"

"He wasn't a Judas. Like Bromwell."

Brandon Jarrett, after days of fine dining and drinking in Atlanta while spending as little time as possible at the actual Convention, is home in Kentucky watching his party's nominee. He changes the channel.

Kati Case watches the whole thing, taking notes. She puts her other notes, about graduate study programs, in a file folder and finishes packing for Boston.

Chapter 53

On Monday night, the Red Sox rally in the eighth inning to defeat the Blue Jays. Kati Case, in a box on the first base side behind the Boston dugout, remarks to Mike Bloom that as much as you've heard, or seen it on TV, it's remarkable how close that big green wall in left field really is.

On Tuesday night, 9 p.m. Eastern time, she walks to the podium to address the Convention. She wonders, will anyone pay attention? The Convention has a depressing Bromwell hangover, until now it's dead in the water. Kati has the very problematical task of waking it up.

After the Beveridge article goes viral, Kati Case, while hardly a household name, has a rising profile. Lauren Baxter helps a lot, pitching on a nightly basis how "this young Pennsylvania Rep is an electrifying presence and symbolic of the forward-thinking direction of the Democratic Party. And an inspiration, and role model, for young women. And ones who aren't so young."

Beveridge himself appears never to be coming back. Having broken what's being described as the biggest story in the history of journalism, The London World Chronicle decides to reward him by keeping him in London. And he's now being asked by his old Oxford dean if perhaps he might be able to teach one of his old courses in the Fall -- with an eye to a permanent return.

Kati tells Lauren Baxter she's sorry all this seems to be costing her a boyfriend. "It's pretty much run its course anyway," she replies. "And you know what they say about streetcars." "I've heard that one," Kati tells her.

Through the TV lights, Kati can make out only a mass of indiscernible bodies, holding up signs and whatnot, stretching the length of the TD Garden. Four years ago, in Baltimore, she was working back rooms.

With the Convention, as one pundit describes it, "mired in malaise, with speakers tiptoeing around the Bromwell problem" -- which Villar continues to rant about -- Kati, the first speaker from the

Burnett inner circle, decides to take it on. "I'll be the lightning rod," she says. Malcolm Douglas agrees. OK with me says Wilson Burnett.

"Let's get one thing straight," she starts out, "I'm not here to apologize about Daniel Bromwell. He wasn't my idea. Four years ago, I was working for a far better candidate -- who happened to be my father."

That starts a "Case, Case, Case" chant in the Pennsylvania delegation. Him or me, she wonders. At least they're awake.

She resumes. "Daniel Bromwell wasn't my idea. He wasn't Wilson Burnett's idea. He wasn't Malcolm Douglas's idea. And for all of you out there who supported him, you had no way -- I repeat, absolutely no way -- of knowing. So what happened wasn't your idea either. And don't let anyone -- especially our opponent -- tell you different."

That gets a big ovation. Possibly they're alive out there.

She turns up the volume. "So just to be 100 per cent clear, I don't know where Mr. Bromwell is. But I know where he isn't. He isn't here. And he isn't the nominee. And that's that.

"The simple truth is, our opponent -- and let's be real about this -- has nothing to say except to demagogue something that nobody -- and I mean nobody -- running against him is responsible for. Why? Because all else he has is the same warmed over and discredited garbage the Republicans have served up for years, with a couple of nutty thoughts of his own added to liven things up and try to make him look like a great innovator. What nonsense."

Guillermo Villar, watching at home on TV, turns to his wife with a laugh. "This one's good, isn't she? She understands where all the bullshit's coming from and isn't afraid to say so."

"As long as you understand, Willie," she tells him.

"Don't worry, I keep things real. Up here." He points to his head.

In Kentucky, in a living room filled with the heads of dead animals shot and generously provided by Beaufort Weatherill, Brandon Jarrett is watching the Democrats for the first time.

"Hey," he says, "she's on a roll."

"You suddenly need to watch when the Case bitch shows up?" his wife says. "Put back Law and Order. And you and her, y'all better not be fuckin'."

Kati waits for the cheers to die down, then launches into a point-by-point repudiation of the Republican platform, compared to the Burnett positions that she and Mike Bloom have crafted. "I suppose," she sums up, "if you want someone who thinks it's fine for people to not go to the doctor because they can't afford it, for people to be starving and homeless, for people scraping along from paycheck to paycheck to pay more taxes than billionaires, then you want Villar and the Republicans. If you want to lock down our country, in violation of our greatest traditions -- even though your own family's been immigrants themselves, and how sick is that? -- you want Villar. If you think our planet will be saved for your children and grandchildren by building dikes, you want Villar. But if you want common sense, fairness and compassion, you want Wilson Burnett and Malcolm Douglas."

More cheering. It's "Kati, Kati, Kati" now. Am I really this electrifying presence Lauren Baxter's been talking about, Kati wonders. She pushes back her hair and waves, to no one she can see, until it dies down. The gender card's never been part of her playbook, but she's decided to go with what Lauren's been pushing. "Thanks so much," she says. "There's one thing I left out. If you want old men to tell women what they can do about their bodies, you want Villar and the Republicans." Cheers again. "And here's why I left that for last. I remember a young girl, nine or ten, in a family that was focused on politics and government, watching one of these conventions on TV. And her mother said, 'one day, that could be you, if you want it.'" (Did Lenore say that? Kati can't recall it.) "I was that girl. And here I am, standing up here today. So if there are other girls out there, or young women, or old women, keep it in mind: if you want it, go get it. And the way to get it is to reject Villar and his stale Republican friends, and support the Burnett campaign." Loud applause. More waves. A big Kati smile. Off she goes.

Mike Bloom gives her a big hug. "It just may be you're a star," he says. "Who'd have thought? Actually, I would've. But that story about your mother?"

"Pure bullshit," she tells him.

Back at The Liberty, in one of the suites transferred by the DNC from the Bromwell campaign, Wilson Burnett and Malcolm Douglas think it's worth high fives. "A real comer, that one," says Glenda Douglas.

At the TruNews desk on the Convention floor, Lauren Baxter tells her viewers "You've just heard the incredibly charismatic Kati Case awaken and reenergize a previously moribund Democratic convention. It was a speech, like Obama's in 2004, that will make her a national figure. And one we'll remember."

In Coral Gables, Guillermo Villar says, "I'm glad the other ones aren't that good."

Back in his old Kentucky home, Brandon Jarrett clicks the remote back to Law and Order. "Finally," Andrea complains. "And she isn't even all that pretty, if you ask me." He walks to the bathroom. Safely inside, he sends a text: "Great, sweet thing" is all it says.

In his Kalorama townhouse, Carter Howell sips his nightly Courvoisier and smiles. He also sends a text: "I'm not always right about things, but I'm right about you."

In Lakotah Lake, North Dakota, Randy Carraway is watching Searching for Bigfoot.

Chapter 54

With the Convention in Boston, Amber Burnett, who's feeling much better, escapes for an afternoon and goes home to Brookline. Her folks are getting old, but they're active and generally OK. Jonathan, her younger brother, the one who took a respectable path and became an accountant, stops by. Alice Rosenfeld is long gone, but you can't completely convince the family of that.

Despite "breaking their hearts" by dropping out and migrating West, she now has a genuine prospect of becoming First Lady. Boy, does that change things. But are they going to let on that he's married to a Jew? (Even if they couldn't ever get her to observe -- she hasn't been in synagogue since her Bat Mitzvah.) It didn't help Dukakis, and they came from Brookline too. Villar's wife is also, she reassures them, so it's not an issue.

She'd rather not have any First Lady talk. Bad luck, she says, but the fact is it's something she doesn't want to even think about. But then, who knows, will she still be married?

She isn't getting any signals from Wilson that he's thinking of leaving. He keeps talking about what it might be like for them living in the White House.

Of course, she can't compete with someone like Kati Case. Maybe she could've given her a run at Kati's age -- even after the two kids she was pretty hot and didn't lack for admirers. But she's comfortably ready for middle-age now, and that's that.

How would it be on her own? They say a woman, abandoned for a younger prospect, is a sad case. But she'd have money, she has a nice circle of friends, she's been largely on her own anyway since Wilson went to the Senate and she mostly stayed home. And she has her admirers, still. She'd survive.

But she'd like to know, one way or the other. So that night, as they're preparing for bed, she says, "this may not be the best time, but I keep wondering if we're getting divorced."

"Who said we were?" he asks.

"Well you have been sleeping with this exciting hot younger woman. I don't blame you, and I let you go to Washington by yourself, so what would anyone expect? And if you want a divorce, I'm not going to fight it, I'm sure I'll be well provided for, as they say. I would like to know, though."

He smiles. "We've been married for a long time. We've had some ups and downs, and some, er, flirtations, but we're still here. And we probably should keep it that way. And Kati, I doubt, really, that she sees me as a permanent thing. So my guess is, you're stuck with me. If that's alright."

She gives him a squeeze on the forearm. "I can live with it."

*   *   *

The speeches are done, a hell-raiser from Malcolm Douglas, a presidential performance from Wilson Burnett that gets generally favorable reviews. Workers are cleaning up balloons and confetti from the TD Garden floor as, accompanied by Vince Lamont, Lanny Feldbaum walks free.

He apparently is telling the truth, the F.B.I. believes he really knew nothing. Has no idea where Bromwell might be. No evidence seems to exist of his involvement. But just to be sure, they confiscate his passport.

That's fine with Lanny Feldbaum, who has no intention of going anywhere but to Chicago. Besides convincing the Feds to let his client go, Vince Lamont has negotiated him out of his DC lease and has been working the phones to set him up back in his hometown. Feldbaum has lots of connections, before long someone's going to decide to make use of them. In the meantime, he'll be staying in Lamont's basement.

Vince Lamont goes back a long time with Feldbaum and Bromwell. "Danny, he wasn't the brightest bulb in the pack, but he was always pretty much the straight arrow," he comments, "at least by local standards. And except for the women. I never would've guessed."

"Or that he could pull off something like that. By himself," Feldbaum answers. "Of course, he did get it fucked up in the end."

"Wonder where he is?"
"Some place warm's my guess."
"Or with Jimmy Hoffa," Lamont says.

Chapter 55

"That speech. She'd be so proud of you, Kaitlyn."

"I guess. Along with letting me know exactly how I   could've made it better."

"Probably."

"Actually, she'd have been offering suggestions in advance."

"I can see that."

"It's nice down here. I like LBI more, but the Bay is good. Guess I can't stay as long as I thought, though."

"What are your plans?"

"Well first I have to go home and see Grandma Angela and Pop Joe. I promised when I thought I'd be having plenty of time"

"Yes. Go. How are they doing? Is he still in the store?"

"Joey Junior's running it, but Grandma and Pop come down for a couple of hours. Pop says the only way he's leaving is with the undertaker."

"I'm sorry my folks weren't around to see."

"Or to see you as Chief Justice."

"Do you have polling?"

"Mixed bag. Villar got a big boost from the Bromwell scandal and their Convention. We've recovered some, but it's an uphill fight I think."

"I think Douglas is a big help. And they're lucky to have you."

"People keep saying that. But I don't know how many votes it's worth."

"Probably best to kick back for a bit. Let's take the boat out."

Chapter 56

Ohio, Pennsylvania, Michigan, Wisconsin, Minnesota, Virginia, North Carolina, Georgia, Texas, Arizona, Nevada -- the usual states, possibly in play, that will be decisive in the ultimate Electoral College count. Not Florida this time, not with Villar running. The candidates criss-cross through them, along with Vice Presidential picks and surrogates. Surrogates are a problem for the Burnett campaign. Anyone with any connection to Bromwell -- and how many Democrats can avoid that -- carries a taint that Villar isn't hesitant to exploit. So more than ever, it falls to Wilson Burnett, Malcolm Douglas, and Kati Case.

Kati finds she's gradually taking on celebrity status. The Convention speech helps, but mainly for voters actually paying attention. Never underestimate how oblivious the masses can be, Carter Howell once told her, and the fact is, many just vaguely remember the name Case from four years before and are trying to piece together who this person might be.

She has her reservations about this phenomenon, a youngish woman with the "movie star looks" the press keeps harping on. Could we just substitute Keira Knightly -- she doesn't look all that different, she's even prettier and skinnier -- have her put on an American accent to read the speeches, and do just as well, Kati wonders. Wilson probably knows her.

But she soldiers on, giving her speeches and interviews, sucking up to local leaders, distributing funds for get-out-the-vote efforts, and thinking how the general public must be getting so sick of all this. She even detours to New Hampshire -- who knows if those four electoral votes will prove important -- and is joined at a rally by the Governor, her supposed husband. They talk, amicably enough, for five minutes.

All over the country, she talks at people but speaks with no one. Except loyal Sheryl Sheldon, who proves to be invaluable in her willingness to do whatever's necessary to keep Kati functional. "Did you really sign up for this," Kati asks when at 4 a.m, Sheryl comes back from an all-night diner in Phoenix with chili and coffee, after they realize that neither of them has eaten for 16 hours. "Not exactly," Sheryl answers, "but you can't say it's not an experience. And eat fast, we have to get to the airport."

Kati sees the two candidates not at all, they connect by conference calls and that's about it. She realizes that her heart is not longing for Wilson Burnett. He's nice to have around, she's quite fond of him. But. I grew up an only child, Kati has always thought, it makes it easier to be on your own. And it didn't take long with Sam Jensen to decide that marriage isn't for Kati Case, even before he made his big confession. Permanency, it seems, is for other people. Anyway, there's no time to be wasted on angst about personal relationships.

In mid-September, they get together in Los Angeles to prep for the first of the two scheduled debates. Burnett's at home, Kati's back in a hotel. Villar retreats to Miami to get ready.

The results of the debate are inconclusive. Villar rants about Bromwell and about Democrats' irresponsible spending. Burnett attacks Villar's demagoguery, tired Republican ideas, and crazy proposals. Nothing different than what they've been saying since July. The polls don't move.

Pollsters, Roger Newley reports, are perplexed. It's difficult enough to poll accurately nowadays, with landlines disappearing, people refusing to take calls from unknown numbers on cell phones, and who knows what mischief can be wreaked on the internet. This year, with the Bromwell scandal and a wildly atypical Republican candidate, it's even more opaque. So all they can offer is that Bromwell continues to drag Democrats down, although the effect may be slowly dissipating, and as much as twenty per cent appear to remain undecided. The bottom line is that as they head into the homestretch, Villar maintains a lead, but it's still up in the air.

Chapter 57

Reports of Daniel Bromwell sightings come from Tehran, Cairo, Lisbon, Grand Cayman, Kyoto, and Pyongyang. It makes oldsters like Carter Howell remember Patty Hearst. Nobody seems to know where he actually is. Well not quite nobody.

He comes in from sunning himself on the patio. He has a different housekeeper today, the other one must have a day off. She serves him the usual fish and rice concoction. It tastes perhaps a bit off, but doesn't it always. An hour later he's struck with excruciating cramps and shortness of breath, and shortly after he's dead.

The housekeeper calls some people she knows. They bundle up the body in sailcloth, weigh it down heavily, take it several miles out into what indeed is the Indian Ocean, and drop it in.

Word gets to Tel Aviv, where Yitzhak Kohn reads an ultra-confidential communique. He smiles as he walks it to the shredder. Not doing something would have set a truly bad precedent, he thinks.

Chapter 58

MEMO -- CONFIDENTIAL
9/20

TO: BURNETT, DOUGLAS, CASE, BLOOM
FROM: GENTRY
RE: POLLING UPDATE

While caution against excessive optimism is in order, polls seem to be trending in our direction. Voters have short memories, and they appear to gradually be forgetting about Bromwell. The fact that he is nowhere to be found is helpful. Should he turn up, be arrested, etc., we likely would lose ground again.

Senator Burnett continues to maintain his favorablity edge as both candidates become better known. We also are getting some indication of voter uneasiness about Villar, especially among voters describing themselves as "traditional Republican" and "moderate Republican." This well may be attributable to unexpressed bias against an ethnically different candidate, which would not be surprising in this demographic. Our focus groups support this view. Participants are "comfortable" with Burnett, less so with Villar. To some degree, the same trend is occurring with Independents.

A large number of voters remain undecided, unusually so for this point in the race. Therefore, most battleground states are in play. Our decision to not contest Florida appears wise, as Villar continues to hold a large lead there by severely drawing away normally Democratic voters in his home county.

As best we can tell, Senator Burnett has likely moved into a several point lead in the national popular vote for the first time. Although this isn't conclusive of battleground state preferences, we can't help but think it's a positive sign.

Chapter 59

Laurenne s'il te plait le temps est court.
Jesus Leroi

"Speak French?" Lauren Baxter asks her producer.

"A little."

She looks at the smudgy pencil on the sheet of loose-leaf paper. "'Lauren, please the time is short,' or something. Jesus the king."

"For fuck's sake," says Lauren Baxter, "can't they do a better job of screening the damn mail."

Chapter 60

"We should just drive," says Sheryl Sheldon. Kati Case has just finished a big rally in the park at the Triangle, where the Monongahela and Allegheny meet. The rivers are brown but calm. The campaign needs Pittsburgh. Kati's confident she'll produce a massive margin in Philadelphia, but they still need a strong showing in western Pennsylvania to offset all the Republicans in the middle of the state.

Then it's off to Ann Arbor. She's actually going to see Wilson Burnett, live and in person, when they get together at an event designed to wake up the student population -- whose vote may be critical in Michigan, and who so far seem unenthused about another gray-haired white guy. "By the time we get to the airport here, and leave time for check-in and security, and then have to drive from the Detroit airport anyway, it's not worth it. And there's a thunderstorms forecast for this afternoon."

"Your call," Kati tells her.

Kati recognizes the benefit of displaying her pretty young self to the Michigan students, but she isn't without trepidation for this trip. She isn't anxious to run into Merrilyn Burnett. Sheryl assures her, she's talked to her close friend, and she's sure Merrilyn is at least accepting of Kati's relationship with her father. Whatever that is, Kati thinks. Since his profession of love, about which, in retrospect, Kati is somewhat skeptical, she's barely seen the man. To say nothing of what her own feelings are.

This is all exacerbated when Sheryl decides to talk about "relationships" and such as she drives the rental car west on the interstates. Sheryl, Kati knows, has done some serious bonding, not surprising since they've been together non-stop for months now, and has come to see her as a sagacious older sister. Or worse yet, surrogate mother.

"Do you think," she asks, pretty much out of nowhere, "that a woman can do what you're doing, or just have any high-powered career, and still do all the domestic things we're supposed to do? I mean, it's not like they don't. But can you really be happy?"

Oh shit, the old have-it-all dilemma, Kati thinks, as she considers what advice she's supposed to offer. She ruminates as she wipes off her Ray-Bans. "Maybe I'm not the best person to ask," she finally says. "I don't do domestic very well, I have absolutely no interest in having kids, and I'm hardly a champ at relationships. I have a marriage that didn't make much sense and a bunch of guys who probably qualify more as encounters than anything else. And I've been thinking, maybe I'm just not capable of anything more than part-time."

Sheryl absorbs that and drives on in silence for a while. "Does it, what you said before, are you OK with it?"

Kati's been hoping this topic was finished. "I think we can all find things to be depressed over. Sometimes it takes a while to find out who you are. Then you have to accept it. I'm still working on it." Not much help, she thinks, but it's all I've got.

She likes Sheryl, she doesn't want to screw her up. What do I know, she thinks. "And please, don't take me as a role model," she adds.

She leafs through her polling data for the umpteenth time. The developing pattern -- that Villar is suffering attrition in his own party because they're racist -- is encouraging on one hand and not so appetizing on the other. "I think you're a great role model," Sheryl suddenly says.

Kati shrugs. "Thanks, I guess. But you know what they say about me, be careful."

*　　*　　*

The stage is set up on the Diag, the blocks-wide park in the middle of the Michigan campus. Stuck in traffic and torrential downpours getting past Toledo, it's close to starting when Kati arrives. Wilson Burnett smiles broadly, plainly happy to see her, but of course there can't be any public show of affection. Sheryl brings Merrilyn over, they shake hands. Cool but not unfriendly, Kati thinks. A relief.

A big crowd is assembling. Students, faculty and locals are on the grass and the many intersecting paths. A few brave ones are sitting on the lower branches of trees. Rather than having some politician do it, Mike Bloom successfully argued for the student head of the Michigan College Democrats to introduce Senator Burnett, and she's giving the brief talk she's been working on for days.

Things look good, all in all. And then the ground shifts under their feet.

Behind the curtain that creates a backstage, The Candidate looks at his notes. His vision is suddenly blurred. His left side is strangely numb, his leg is collapsing. He grabs for the folding chair in front of him. "I don't -- " is all he says. Mike Bloom is there first, Ed Williams, the head of the Secret Service detail, right behind. They each support an arm. "The car, fast," Williams shouts.

The black bulletproof SUV is parked on the grass in the open area behind the stage, ready for an emergency. Wilson Burnett is now limp, not clearly conscious, as another Secret Service officer, trained for crises, takes over from Bloom. "A stroke I think," Ed Williams yells. "Time's critical." They bundle the Senator into the car and head off to the hospital, just minutes away.

Kati Case watches in horror. Merrilyn Burnett is sobbing into Sheryl Sheldon's shoulder. Mike Bloom looks like a ghost.

Out front, the head of the College Democrats finishes her introduction. She looks around, but Senator Burnett doesn't emerge. "Go give the speech," Bloom shouts.

Kati doesn't respond. "Get out there and do something," he yells.

"How?" she says.

"Give the damn speech. You wrote it. Or give your speech, just get out there."

Sheryl Sheldon is leading Merrilyn to her car, to follow to the hospital. Kati Case, on autopilot, drifts onto the stage. The crowd expects Wilson Burnett, but they pretty much know who she is. They cheer. She waves and forces herself to put on a politician smile. She can't imagine how she's going to get through this without breaking down.

"Hey," she says into the microphone, "I'm Kati Case." More applause. "Unfortunately, Senator Burnett isn't feeling well, so you're gonna be stuck with me." Out there, they have no idea this looks serious. They've been expecting her to speak at some point, they're unconcerned.

Kati Case gives a speech. She haphazardly mixes her own talking points with what she's written -- and revised as the campaign wore on -- for Wilson Burnett. She fights off the urge to think about anything else. It seems random and incoherent, but they cheer in all the right spots. She gets an ovation at the end. She scarcely hears it. She walks off, sits down in a chair, and collapses, sobbing.

Mike Bloom is standing there. "Sorry," he says, "to make you do that. But if anyone could. Amazing."

She looks up at him. "What did I say? I have no clue. But Wilson?"

"Williams was right. Guess they're trained for this sort of thing. A stroke."

"How bad?"

"Don't know. Let's go to the hospital.

*   *   *

The University of Michigan Medical Center, one of the nation's leading hospitals, has a Comprehensive Stroke Center. Merrilyn Burnett, as next of kin, hears what the doctors can ascertain at this point and returns to pass it on. She's now somewhat composed, but asks Sara Tazaki, Wilson Burnett's exotic looking half-Japanese, half-Portuguese spokesperson, who's been with him since their studio days, to explain.

He's stabilized. A significant stroke. Medically induced coma. Next 48 hours are critical. For survival, she tells them, as her voice breaks.

Tears are running down Mike Bloom's face. Kati grabs his hand as she fights back her own desire to just go ahead and weep.

The prognosis longer term, they can't really tell. Getting him to the hospital so quickly is a positive. But at the least, they're looking at a long period of rehab, for movement, vision, talking. They're hopeful he won't be mentally impaired. But again --

Sheryl, who's managed to hold it together until now to support Merrilyn, dissolves in tears as she hugs Kati.

Amber? Catching a red-eye. Ed Williams is picking her up in Detroit tomorrow morning.

Malcolm Douglas? "I talked to him before, but he doesn't know the details," Mike Bloom says. "I'd better -- "

"I will," Kati says.

He's in a hotel room in Charlotte. He puts his phone on speaker so Glenda can hear. "It's pretty bad," Kati tells him. "They're cautiously optimistic, they say, that he'll pull through. But after that -- " she trails off, sniffling.

She can tell he's been crying too. "We heard it all. It's been all over the news since right after Mike called. Someone in the hospital must have leaked the whole damn thing. My brother-in-law, he went through it. Took him a good year to get going again. Glenda's here. She's been praying."

I wish I could, Kati thinks. "I've got to call Morelli," he adds.

It takes a while, but he calls back. "The press already knows everything. We have to be at DNC tomorrow afternoon."

"I figured. You, I guess. And you have to figure out, Vice President, you know."

"I've been thinking about it. And we've been talking about how to handle it all. But I need you to promise, whatever I say, you'll support it."

"Of course."

"Promise?

"Promise."

Chapter 61

Kati's calls: Lauren Baxter. Juanita Gomez. Carter Howell. Brandon Jarrett. Her father. Sam Jensen. Clement McWillis. Roger Newley. She lets them all ring through to voicemail.

She skims the news on her phone as they sit on the runway. Another unprecedented event. Malcolm Douglas in the spotlight. How will the Vice Presidential candidate be selected? Concern for Senator Burnett and his family from Guillermo Villar, but they've decided against suspending the campaign and his rally in Houston will proceed as scheduled. All heart, she thinks.

Up at cruising altitude, her head drops onto Mike Bloom's shoulder and she dozes off. Neither has slept. He looks down at her and smiles sadly, reflecting on the long trip they've been on since they were little kids, and closes his eyes.

*   *   *

In Washington, Charles Gray, in early, tells his secretary that when Morelli phones, put him right through. Then he calls Carter Howell.

"Awful stuff. But now what? Your thoughts?"

"Of course, the circumstances are less clear than before," Carter Howell says. "Then at least there was the Convention to confirm the result, they just had to free the delegates. Now, it seems to me, they should just make a choice, choose a candidate and running mate, and put it out there. They can't have another Convention, what other way is there?"

"I tend to agree," the attorney replies. "We can't find any legal guidance one way or the other. Do you think they need to poll the Executive Committee? Or the whole DNC? And there's the timing problem, changing ballots and all."

"Absolutely. It needs to be ASAP. Just tell Morelli to sit down with Douglas and get it done. There isn't time to try to herd cats."

204

*   *   *

Walt Morelli phones Charles Gray. "I'd say," the attorney advises, "that you can do whatever you decide. I mean, you can't have another convention. And what's anyone going to do about it?"

"Do I have to convene the Executive Board? Or poll the whole damn Committee?" Morelli asks.

"I'd say the most important thing is, whatever you decide, do it fast. There's ballots to print and machines to change. We may need to go to court in some states. My advice is, anoint Douglas, find a VP he likes, and make an announcement. Fuck the rest, if you'll pardon my French."

*   *   *

By early afternoon, Kati Case and Malcolm Douglas are sitting in Walt Morelli's office. On the walls are photos of Obama, Bill Clinton, JFK, and FDR. There's also an empty space where until recently Bromwell was hanging.

Morelli looks surprised to see Kati. "I think he just expects me," Malcolm told her, "but I'll be damned if I'm going without you."

"Legal counsel says, one, we can do whatever we want, and two, we have to do it damn fast," Morelli starts out. "So we need a VP. Malcolm, it's pretty much your call, right?"

Malcolm Douglas takes a deep breath. "We already have a VP candidate," he says.

Morelli looks puzzled. "Who?"

"Me," he replies.

"You can't run for both."

"Of course not," he says and laughs. "I said from the git go that I wanted no part of being President."

Kati sits there in shock. How can he be doing this?

Morelli slams his fist down. "We need a candidate right away, you can't pull this. If not you, what the fuck can we do?"

Malcolm Douglas smiles calmly and turns toward Kati Case. "Her," is all he says.

Kati opens her mouth. Malcolm holds up one meaty hand toward her, palm outward. "Remember," he tells her. She blinks but says nothing.

"You're kidding, right? We can't possibly," Morelli answers.

"Never been more serious."

"She's too young, too inexperienced, nobody knows her. No."

"Let me tell you something," Malcolm Douglas says, and his voice rises just enough to cause Morelli to sit back. "She's been all over the country, she saved the Convention, she's been the brains behind this whole campaign -- and everyone knows it. And, if you ask me, the heart and soul too. So don't 'no' me."

Morelli looks at Kati as she stares blankly and tries to make sense of what's happening. "You've put him up to this, young lady?"

Big mistake. The "young lady" is just what's needed to piss her off and bring her back to earth. "Hardly," she spits back, "but I support whatever Malcolm says." Which is what he made me promise.

"No," Morelli says again. "I won't have it and that's that. There's someone else out there."

"Maybe you could call in Bromwell again," Kati chimes in.

Morelli turns several shades of red. "This meeting is over," he says before there's a nuclear explosion.

"Not exactly," says Malcolm Douglas, quietly. "Here's how it is, Walt. If she's not the candidate, I'm out. And the word's gonna be, I was disrespected."

"You weren't. You know -- "

"Now, don't interrupt me, sir. As I said, Black folks'll hear I was disrespected. And once they get that, they'll stay home, or maybe even vote Villar. What do you think your chances are then?"

"It's extortion," Morelli sputters.

"It's politics," says Malcolm Douglas.

*   *   *

Kati Case and Malcolm Douglas walk together toward the Capitol down the block. "I'm running for President? How could you? And thanks for the heads-up."

"I figured if I let you know you'd argue."

"Obviously."

"And you promised you'd support what I said, so there it was."

"But why?"

"Because of all I said. Fact is, it's Glenda's idea. After we heard the awful news, we got to talking like you'd expect. About this and that and the pros and cons. About how I really never wanted it, but now, what choice do I have. And she waited 'till the right moment, she's so smart that way, and she said, 'what about Kati. She's the best one to, like they say, pick up the torch.' Convinced me, like she always does."

"I can't quite compute here. Last night. Now this. What am I supposed to be doing."

"Just what we've been doing all along, I expect. Knowing you, you'll get with it fast. First though, we need to call your friend Newley and get the story out the way we want, before Morelli screws it up."

*   *   *

"Kati, I'm so sorry. Are you OK?" Roger Newley asks.

"Not really, but look Roger, I've got a big story for you to break. Maybe not as good as Bromwell, but you'll get an exclusive you can get out right away."

"Shoot."

"I'm the candidate."

"What?"

"Try to control your shock. Malcolm's staying as Vice, I'm running for POTUS."

Roger Newley grabs his recorder. "Can I get some quotes?"

"Absolutely. Malcolm's here too. Here's what we want to say."

*   *   *

"I hear you played some hoops back in the day," Malcolm Douglas says when they get off the phone.

"Yeah, Chuckin' Kati, my coach called me. I just kinda hung out at the three-point line and fired 'em up. I was like 100 pounds, so if I tried to go inside they kicked the crap out of me."

"I played more in the paint," he tells her. "Not big enough though to make it in college. Hey, we could use some unwinding. Want to go to the gym and shoot some up?"

Chapter 62

EAR TO THE GROUND
By Roger Newley

EXCLUSIVE

Formal announcement is expected tomorrow, but The Ear has received exclusive information that the Democratic candidate for President to replace stricken Senator Wilson Burnett will be Pennsylvania Congresswoman Kati Case.

Senator Burnett is now in an Ann Arbor, Michigan, hospital in serious but stable condition after suffering what has been described by doctors as a "significant stroke" just before he was scheduled to speak at a rally last night on the University of Michigan campus. His situation is such, sources tell us, that it would be impossible for him to continue as a candidate.

Representative Case, 37, stepped in as the rally's primary speaker after seeing Senator Burnett taken to the hospital. "I can't image doing anything more difficult than that," she told The Ear.

"It was by every account a remarkable performance," said Ohio Congressman and Vice Presidential candidate Malcolm Douglas, who was expected to take over the Presidential candidacy, but who -- at what he emphasized was entirely his own choice -- instead will remain on the ticket in the second spot. "It shows clearly how cool and collected she is in a crisis, which is so important for being Commander-in-Chief, and she's clearly the one most ready and capable to lead our party and the country," Douglas added.

Ms. Case has come to national attention as a leading surrogate for the Burnett campaign, and for a stirring speech she gave at the Democratic

Convention which has been credited with giving Democrats "life and hope," as one observer put it, after the Bromwell scandal. "The direction of the campaign will not change," she told The Ear. "The things we stood for before, we stand for now: equality, both as to wealth and otherwise, tax reform, alleviating people's concern for healthcare, rights for every gender status, and a foreign policy aimed at peace and fairness. Sadly, we have no choice but to change the name at the top of the ticket, but the goals remain."

Thus far, The Ear has been unable to reach Republican candidate Guillermo Villar for comment.

Chapter 63

"Oh Kaitlyn, I'm so sorry. Are you alright?"

"I guess. I want to tell you before it hits the press. It's me."

"Excuse me?"

"For POTUS."

"No."

"Yes."

"But how? What about Douglas?"

"It's his idea."

"I'm glad I'm sitting down."

"That's all?"

"Well, I thought one day. But not yet. Yet circumstances being what they are, I can see it. If Douglas -- "

"That's how."

"Well, I don't know which way the votes are going to fall, this whole thing is so extraordinary, but if you win, there isn't a doubt in my mind you can do the job."

"Thanks, Dad. Wish Mom were here."

Chapter 64

"How did it go?" Carter Howell asks Malcolm Douglas.

"Pretty much as you orchestrated. It's done."

"Morelli?"

"Somewhere between apoplectic and fit-to-be tied."

"How was Kati?"

"Pretty much in shock. What else can you expect? But then, Morelli, the jerk, set her off by calling her 'young lady'." So she said something like, why don't you call Bromwell again. Morelli turned purple. I had to really work not to laugh."

"How is she now?" Carter Howell asks.

"She's Kati. Walking back to the Capitol, she bitched about not getting a heads-up. By the time we were there, she was figuring out exactly what to tell the press. Then we called her pal Newley, he's breaking it this afternoon like you advised, before Morelli can. And after that, we went to the gym and she beat me three out of four in Horse, took me for ten bucks. The girl can shoot."

"Horse? Sorry, I've never had time to get into sports."

"I'm glad there's at least one thing you don't know about."

"Well anyway, it sounds like it went as well as you can expect, all in all. So good luck. And I'm always here, you know."

* * *

"Hey, sweet thing. You OK?"

"Hanging in. You, Brandon?"

"Just bein' me, sweet thing. Hey, can I call you sweet thing if you're the President?"

"Who said you could now?"

"Come on. Seriously, is there anything I can do for you."

Kati laughs. "The only thing you can do for me isn't happening. Especially since I'm now surrounded by Secret Service. But if I think of anything else, I'll call back."

"OK. And, sweet thing, don't tell anyone, but I'm rooting for you. And I kinda miss you."

*　　*　　*

"Oh Juanita, thanks for calling before, sorry I couldn't get back -- "

"No need. How are you?"

"Doing better. It's good to have something to get focused on."

"It's a pretty big something you've got. So, I talked to Amber a little while ago."

"And?"

"He's still stable. That's good. They're going to start bringing him out tomorrow, from the sedation. Then, it's a long haul ahead. So sad."

"Yeah. How's Amber?"

"Taking charge. She's tough like you. She'll manage. She's going to call you when things settle down. And another thing."

"Yes?"

"You know, I was going to be involved. But now I'm trying to clear my calendar for pretty much all of October. Any states where you need someone to speak Spanish, I'm there."

"Thanks. Much."

"And you'd be surprised what I'm hearing. The Republicans don't get it, they think all Latinos are alike. But the Mexicans, and the Puerto Ricans, and the people from Central America, or the Dominican, they don't necessarily trust the Cubans so much, they're not going to vote for some guy just because he speaks some Spanish, and not too well. So there's lots of votes out there."

Kati sighs. "No one likes anyone else, do they. Kind of sad, isn't it."

"Welcome to America, amigo."

*　　*　　*

"I suppose we need to get divorced after all if you win."

"You finally get it?"

"I don't feature being First Lady."

"No," she laughs, "you'd be shit at that."

*   *   *

"I'm so sorry for all this, but for an old man whose time is short, I'm glad to be able to see you go for it. I knew you would someday."

"Stop the old man crap. You'll outlast all of us. But, do you think I actually can win."

"In politics they say the only thing that's predictable is that it's unpredictable, or some such. This year is so bizarre, I'm done even guessing. You have to catch up on name recognition and all, and there isn't much time. But I think Villar's support is soft. Any polling?"

"Not yet."

"Well even if you lose, you're well positioned for the next time."

"Carter, please."

*   *   *

"You need to be back on the show. I'll give you the whole hour."

"Definitely. Hey, I was meaning to ask you. With Rupert gone, do you think you'd be interested in my father? He can be kind of stiff, but after Beveridge -- "

"Interesting idea."

*   *   *

"That slut Kati Case's runnin' for President now? Guess she'll be too busy for y'all to be fuckin', eh Brandon."

Chapter 65

Guillermo Villar meets with his team. Optimism reigns. Of course, we'd never wish this on anyone, they agree. Although probably they would, if it means regaining the White House. And now, they unfortunately can't start putting out the word that Wilson Burnett and Kati Case are much more than political allies like they'd planned. It would have been a safe play, since Villar himself is scrupulously monogamous -- unlike Bromwell, departed but hardly forgotten, especially in the standard Villar campaign speech. But no, now voters would find it a sleazy and tasteless move.

Despite her relatively enhanced profile, you can't drop a 37-year-old House member with still-limited national name recognition into a presidential race with little more than a month to go, his pollsters contend. Early surveys, they say, support their view. Voters have been hearing from Villar for months. They'll be more comfortable with someone they know.

She makes me nervous, Villar says, even my wife really admires her. Of course, she was once a Democrat. Don't worry, he's told. It's in the bag.

They'd like an excuse to skip the October debate. Why give her the opportunity to let voters see her? Did it hurt Bromwell to duck debating? Not apparently. Certainly not as much as being paid off by Iran. Villar agrees. Figure out how to do it, he tells them.

*   *   *

Wally Gentry meets in-person and has sobering news for the newly-minted Case campaign. While Senator Burnett had surged to a small lead in national polling, 46-43, with 11 percent still undecided, Villar now leads Case by 45-38. Obviously, significant Burnett support had slipped into undecided, with voters attempting to cope with a new candidate as the race enters the homestretch. Battleground state numbers are generally tracking the national polling, Gentry concludes.

Wally Gentry is a numbers-nerd who previously worked for Wilson Burnett projecting movie revenues. A Berkeley Phi Beta Kappa, he defies the numbers-nerd stereotype and instead still looks like he's in Hollywood, with blond hair long but neat, carefully pressed slacks and sports shirts, and contacts rather than thick glasses. Currently he's sleeping with a cute dark-haired starlet who's hoping to graduate from B movies. Kati Case has picked up signals that he'd be interested, but she isn't. Not my type.

"The only remedy," he offers to Kati, Malcolm Douglas, and Mike Bloom, "is to get out there. I don't think there's been that much real movement to Villar, so what we need is to persuade the significant cohort that's become unsettled and confused by Senator Burnett's dropping out. Kati really needs to kill it in the debate. And Malcolm absolutely needs to motivate the African-American vote, we need the turnout."

"Got it," Kati says. "Focus groups?"

"Next week."

Kati takes Bloom aside. "What about Sheryl?" she asks. "Now that I've inherited you and the candidate staff, she's kind of redundant. But she's worked so hard -- "

"Bring her. We can find things for her to do."

"Thought you'd say that."

*   *   *

Kati Case is in an Oval Office armchair. Clement McWillis sits at the Resolute Desk. All the Bromwell memorabilia is still around. "You don't go redecoratin' a short-term rental," he tells people.

He hauls his considerable bulk out of the large red leather desk chair. "Want to try it out?" he asks. "Nah, that'd be bad luck. But sittin' there, I don't cotton to it t'all." He walks over and plops down in a chair next to Kati. "Not like I got that much I'm doin.'"

"We think you could help," she tells him. "There's places we have a chance, North Carolina, Georgia, Texas, where maybe you could move some white voters."

"Throw some corn pone at 'em, I'd be glad to. May not know much about what I'm doin' here, but I surely can still talk. And some folks down there, sad to say, but I suspect they don't feel good 'bout a feller with a funny name talkin' Spanish. Might like to hear from someone talks like me."

Kati frowns. "I hate it, you know. Thinking we have to rely on people's prejudice."

He slaps his hand on his thick leg. "Growin' up in the deepest South, I know all about it. I grew up dirt poor, my best friends were Black boys and I took plenty of shit for it, pardon my language. But you can't change folks who don't want changin', it's been a long time and we've got quite a ways to go. Just so's you're not doin' things that make it worse. And when you can, you try to make it better."

"I'm glad I'm getting to know you, Mr. Pres -- Clem."

"Why thank you, miss, I feel honored on my part, truly. And one more thing. When Senator Burnett's ready to go home, Air Force One's at his disposal. Don't give a damn if anyone complains."

*　　*　　*

"They say he's out of danger," Amber Burnett tells Kati. "He has some movement on his left side, which they say is good. Talking's pretty hard, but we got him a board and he can write. His right hand's fine."

"How's, you know -- ?"

"His mind? He sleeps a lot, but he pretty much knows what's going on. I told him about what's happened. He wrote something for you: 'Tell her I'm not surprised. And that's she's going to win.'"

Kati is perceptibly crying. "And you?"

"It'll be rough. I'm not kidding myself. But I'm OK, you know, you do what you need to do. You can't tell what's coming around the next corner. You just put on your turn signal and hope for the best. 'Cause accidents happen, and sometimes you can't do a thing about it. Except deal with it."

"I wish -- " Kati sniffles.

"Stop. Right now, you just go and take care of business. There's nothing that'd make him happier."

Chapter 66

Flying from Las Vegas to Houston on the campaign plane, now repainted with "Kati Case" in giant red and blue letters on the side, she and Mike Bloom are up front talking about the upcoming debate. And whether Villar will duck it.

Sheryl Sheldon comes by from the rear. "You back there still crushing on the Secret Service dude," Kati teases her.

"Nah," she says with a grin. "He's hot enough. But he doesn't have much to say. I'm waiting on Bloom's conversion therapy. So what's up?"

"Just talking debate stuff," Bloom says. "Wondering if there's going to be one."

"Yeah, she says, I've been hearing he's gonna chicken out."

"You've been hearing?" Kati asks.

"I get around. I mean, why would he want to give you all that exposure, considering it's, like, your biggest problem."

"True," says Bloom.

"But I was thinking," Sheryl goes on. "Maybe this is just stupid, but, remember that web ad with the chicken head we used when Bromwell wouldn't show?"

"That didn't do much good," Kati says.

"Well what about this. If he says he's not showing up, what it we buy like an hour of prime time and you answer questions people send in. And next to you we set up a chair with a guy in a chicken suit wearing a sign that says 'Villar'?"

Kati looks at Bloom. Bloom looks at Kati. "Interesting," she says. "Crazy. But interesting."

Sheryl Sheldon retreats to the rear. "The girl has a future in politics," Mike Bloom says.

"That's what I'm afraid of," Kati replies.

*   *   *

Lanny Feldbaum calls Kati Case. She declines the call. She asks Sheryl Sheldon, now elevated to assistant to Mike Bloom, to call him back.

"This is what he says," she reports. "He says he's still a loyal Democrat, and he's going to work for some council guy in Chicago. And they had some research on Villar, about some golf course development he supposedly got paid off for years ago, before he was even Mayor. We can have it."

Kati rolls her eyes. "Tell him we'll get back to him."

*   *   *

In Phoenix, Juanita Gomez tells a crowd that's largely Mexican that Villar is a fraud. "Don't be fooled. He's less Latinx than Kati Case. She took two years of Spanish in college, and a course in Latino culture, and that's more than he knows. Just listen to him, his Spanish sucks, if you'll pardon me for saying so. I'll bet he has it written out for him phonetically. His family's been rich in Florida with the other rich Cubans for years, he's clueless about your experience, and he couldn't care less."

"She doesn't mess around, does she," says Mike Bloom as they watch the TV coverage.

"That's how she got where she is," says Kati.

*   *   *

Malcolm Douglas works North Carolina, Georgia, Cleveland, Detroit and Milwaukee. "Don't be fooled," he also says. "Just because his skin is a little on the darker side, he isn't like you. He's a Republican and he doesn't give a damn about poor folks and folks of color. Vote, vote vote, you need to get out and vote."

"Do you think," Kati asks, "that maybe we're pushing the demographics too much?"

Bloom shrugs. "Gentry said to," he answers.

Chapter 67

On a drizzly night in Missoula, Vernon Russell is studying for his Organic Chemistry midterm. A full-blooded Cheyenne, he's managed to overcome eighty per cent hearing loss from childhood measles to become the first member of his family to attend college, at the University of Montana. Next year he hopes to start medical school. He leaves his apartment and goes to a nearby convenience store. With a long night ahead, he gets a Red Bull and a turkey sandwich, and scrolls through emails on his phone as Sid James at the register fetches the sandwich. He puts his phone down to pay, and, thinking about Organic Chemistry, forgets it on the counter. As he walks away down the block, Sid James notices and runs out. Vernon Russell is well off by then, and Sid James yells "Stop, stop," as he chases after him through the mist.

Merritt Fulton, with eleven years on the Missoula police force, drives by on routine patrol. He evaluates the situation, sees a guy in a convenience store outfit chasing one of the few dark-skinned individuals in Missoula, figures he's come upon the aftermath of a robbery, rolls down his window, and yells "halt now, police."

Vernon Russell can hear neither of them and keeps on going. Merritt Fulton has a sinus headache, and is pissed off that he's being disregarded. He stops the cruiser, jumps out, steps in a puddle, yells "halt police" one more time, gets no response, and shoots Vernon Russell in the back. He calls for an ambulance as Sid James rushes up and explains. "God no," he says and sinks to his knees. Vernon Russell undergoes emergency surgery and is expected to survive, but will be paralyzed from the waist down.

It takes a few days for the whole story to trickle out. Guillermo Villar consults with his advisers, is told he can't risk losing pro-police white voters, and issues a statement that "despite this unfortunate incident, we fully support local police and the difficult split-second decisions they need to make every day." Native American activists are up in arms, but, as usual, hardly anyone pays attention. "Since we allowed genocide and stealing their land," Kati Case says to Malcolm

Douglas, "I guess one more kid isn't going to matter much." What she says to the press is that her father was a prosecutor, she appreciates how tough it can be for police on the front lines, but the unwarranted carnage of people of color needs to stop. And she decides to go to Missoula.

You can't cancel appearances in battleground states to go to Montana, where you have no chance of winning, on behalf of Native Americans, not enough of whom vote anyway, everyone tells her. Kati mentions her framed RFK poster, and how he took time out from his presidential campaign to go to the Pine Ridge reservation in South Dakota against the counsel of his advisers. "I'm no idealist," she says, "anyone who knows me knows that, and I'm pragmatic and political and all that shit, and I'm certainly no Bobby Kennedy either, but once in a while you have to do something for no better reason that you think it's right."

"And once you get an idea in your head, that's kind of the end of it," Mike Bloom points out.

"She should go," says Malcolm Douglas.

The press meets her plane when it lands in Missoula. "No questions," Kati says, "this isn't a campaign stop."

She visits Vernon Russell in the hospital. Now that I'm here, she wonders, what am I supposed to do? He's still pretty drugged up, but he knows who she is. His parents have driven down from the reservation. They probably aren't much older than Kati, but they look twice her age. His mother starts sobbing when Kati comes in.

She makes small talk. Vernon Russell asks her how the election's going. His mother tells about how hard Vernon's always worked. His father is largely silent.

"Why would he do that?" his mother finally asks. "He had no reason. Now look."

"I'm sorry I can't do more," Kati offers, "people make bad decisions. And I'd be lying if I told you that if he, your boy, had light skin, it would've been the same thing."

"He had his whole life ahead. Now what?"

"All I can tell you is this. He can't give up." She looks at Vernon. He nods back. "What's happened, you can overcome it, I promise. I'm sure the University's going to work something out. And if you need help with anything, let me know. Win or lose, let me know."

His mother looks at Ed Williams. "Am I allowed to hug her?" she asks. He nods yes and they embrace.

Outside, Kati asks if she can visit the cop. Ed Williams calls ahead.

Merritt Fulton is maybe 45. He's dressed in old black sweatpants and a plain white t-shirt, his hair is short and graying, and he looks like he hasn't shaved for days. He lives in a one-bedroom walk-up. His wife and three kids left years ago for Oregon. He hasn't bothered to clean up, there's a couple of dirty shirts, pants, and some boxers on the floor, the sink is full of unwashed dishes, the recycling bin is overflowing with Miller Lite cans and a bottle of Gordon's Gin.

He tells Ed Williams he isn't interested. On the nightstand in his bedroom is his service revolver, which is empty now except for one bullet he's thinking of using. In eleven years on the force, he'd never fired it once excepting at the range.

His lawyer told him he won't go to jail. "Officers rarely get convicted, they may not even prosecute. Juries have let worse stuff go than what you did. I'll work with the union to get you reinstated once it all dies down." Nobody's told him how he's supposed to live with it, but he can't imagine how some East-coast lefty like Kati Case is going to help.

Driving to the airport, Ed Williams asks Kati what she was thinking of saying to Merritt Fulton. She just shrugs. "Yeah," he says, "sometimes there's not much you can do, well intentioned as you are. But you should be proud of yourself for coming."

Chapter 68

Villar announces that his schedule won't permit him to debate. And that "sources" who are "in direct contact" with Cuban officials tell him that the Cubans are "so enthusiastic" about becoming the 51st state.

The Case campaign implements Operation Chicken. For an hour in prime time, the highly telegenic candidate, wearing a modest navy pants suit, fields questions texted and emailed from voters across the country. Screened, of course, but they allow some tougher ones to make it look more legit. The chicken, wearing its Villar sign, sits quietly beside her.

"Ms. Case, you're quite young, you've only been in the Congress for a short time, and you have no executive experience. How can we trust you to lead the nation?"

"Thank you for your question. I'm sure many Americans wonder about that. I think what's in your head and heart is what counts, not what's on paper as your supposed experience. And what you stand for. Remember too, I've been in Congress for six years now. My opponent has no experience in federal government, and aside from some completely unworkable proposals, represents only tired ideas of the past that his party has been peddling for years. Of course, it would be nice if he were here to discuss them." She points to the chicken. "But sadly, he doesn't have enough respect for you to show up." She smiles sweetly. "Next question?"

"Ms. Case, Mayor Villar has an innovative plan to end our long-standing disputes with Cuba by joining them to our country, and he says Cuba wants to. Isn't that a good idea?"

"Thank you for your question. Well, wouldn't it be nice if he were here to explain it." Gestures toward chicken. "I don't think it stands a chance of happening, and frankly I simply don't believe what he says about a mysterious unnamed source who's supposedly been in contact with Cuba -- which, by the way, would be highly improper, if you ask me. We have far more important things to worry about, as I've been discussing." She smiles sweetly.

It goes on like that. She calmly responds over and over with the talking points she's been harping on for weeks, which isn't all that different from what she'd be doing if there were an actual debate. She smiles prettily a lot. The chicken plays a significant, if silent, role almost every time.

At eleven, ten Central, local news invariably shows Kati clips, with chicken close-ups. The next day, Lauren Baxter opines that "Kati Case killed it, and brilliantly showed that Villar is all about being chicken sh -- Oh, better not." She also tells her audience that she's excited to announce that Kati will be on live for an hour very soon.

In a hotel room in Detroit, Guillermo Villar fumes. "Who thought this was a good idea?" he grumps.

Overnight national Poll:

VILLAR 45
CASE 41
UNDECIDED 14

Chapter 69

Lauren Baxter starts her hour-long sit-down with Kati Case by mentioning that Guillermo Villar has, of course, also been invited for his own session, but hasn't responded. "Cluck, cluck, cluck," she adds.

They save the Bloody Mary pitcher for afterwards. "I can drink as much as I want now," Kati laughs, "Secret Service chauffeurs me everywhere."

"Your Dad called me," Lauren tells her. "We had a nice dinner."

"And?"

"Seems like a nice man. Good looking. Kind of on the stodgy side. And a perfect gentleman, he dropped me off, said goodnight, and left. No moves at all. Think he's just not interested?"

"He probably thinks my Mother's watching. It's been like 16 years, and he hasn't had a decent relationship. It's all I can do to get him out of the house. But don't give up. He loosens up after a while. I'll keep after him if you want."

"Yeah. Let's keep trying."

Kati sighs. "It's so tiresome. And kind of ridiculous. We do the damn focus groups so they can tell me I have to sit there and be a good girl, but be tough, and criticize but not too nasty, and wear modest outfits and look good so the guys are interested, but not too good so the women don't get pissed off when their husbands suddenly insist on watching the news. This is how we pick the leader of the free world?"

"Of course if you had a penis, you'd just show up in a suit and run your mouth however you want. But we've known that."

Kati closes her eyes and leans back. "Oh well. No one made me do this. Well, Douglas did, actually, but he's the last guy I'd get mad at." She looks over and Lauren Baxter is sobbing. "Lauren ?"

"I was raped," is all she says.

"My God. How? Who?"

"No," Lauren responds, wiping her eyes, "a long time ago, when I first moved here, when I was still at the RNC. I've never said a word, to anyone."

"Do you want to talk about it?" Kati says and walks over to where she's sitting. Lauren stands up and they hug.

"I was working late, and this guy came in. A governor from a very red state in the middle of the country. He's been dead for a while. Didn't say a word, came up behind where I was sitting, kissed me on the back of the neck, yanked me out of my chair and backed me against a wall, pulled up my skirt and ripped down my panties, and did it. 'Thanks,' he said as he zipped up, and he just walked out.

"I went home and pretty much stayed in bed for days. I called in and said I had the flu. I went back but I couldn't stand being in the office. I got my resume together, and that's how I wound up in television."

They both sit back down. "And you never?"

"Not a word. You know, did I really have a choice? If I said anything, it would've been the end of any career I had, and they'd have said I was crazy and lying and everything. And then he was dead. It's not like I was the only one. Did you?"

"Thank God, no," Kati says. "I think guys are kind of afraid of me. The worst that ever happened was in high school, I thought my tennis coach was copping feels while he was showing me how to fix my backhand. I finally pulled away and told him that if he didn't stop, I'd kick him in the nuts so hard he'd be a eunuch, and my mother would do worse. That was the end of it, he decided to live with my crappy backhand."

"Thanks for making me laugh. And you wonder why they might be afraid of you? Anyway, I'm glad I finally told someone. I mean, I still have nightmares once in a while, but I don't think I'm crazier than anyone else around here."

"Can I ask you? I mean, we've become pretty tight, but you don't know me all that long. So why me?"

"You know, I'm not so sure myself. I'm friendly with a lot of people, but I don't really have close friends."

"Sounds familiar."

"Yeah, I thought so. Then, when you made that trip to Montana just because you decided it was something you should do, and everyone said you were nuts, I thought, if she did that, she really has something going for her. I've always thought that part of what presidents do is being a kind of national psychiatrist, the good ones anyway, so here I am, your first patient."

"I'm not president. And I have issues enough myself," Kati says. "Maybe you can just be my older sister."

"As long as you don't stress the older part. And be careful what you wish for. I have one, for years she made me miserable. She once told me, 'you're like dog shit on the bottom of my shoe.' She got better. But she's still a Republican."

*   *   *

Next morning, first thing, Kati is behind the desk at her Longworth Building office when Brandon Jarrett stops by and closes the door. "Early for you, no?" she says.

"Figured it's the only way to catch you. Heard you'd be around."

"Just faking like I'm a functioning member of Congress for a morning."

"Hardly a problem. I've been doing it for years." He walks over, bends down, and gives her a serious kiss on the mouth.

"Damn," says Kati. "You asshole," she adds -- although it's hard not to notice several body parts are awakening from a period of dormancy.

She stands up. He puts his hands up, like he thinks she's planning to whack him one. Instead she pulls him close and kisses him back. "OK," she says, "that's out of the way." She sits back down.

"So what're you thinking," he says, shaking his head as he takes a seat. "What's your polling?"

She raises her hands, palms up. "Slowly improving but we have so little time, and with it all, not enough people know who the hell I am. They're already voting, although it looks like the early voting's comparatively light because things are so unsettled, they don't know what to do. Still, there's this huge Republican vote that's going to support their candidate regardless."

"No kidding. How do you think I keep getting re-elected."

"Oh, you're not so bad," Kati says, smiling. "I just feel like we're swimming against the tide here, but what can you do."

"You know, there's folks on my side of the aisle that don't think much of him either, your opponent. Especially after Bromwell, they'd prefer somebody who seems more stable, and without the bullshit." He looks at his watch. "You going over?"

They take the short walk to the Capitol flanked by Ed Williams and the agent Sheryl Sheldon thinks is hot and go into the large Hall in the south wing where the House meets. Kati draws lots of attention, while Brandon Jarrett slips over to his side largely unnoticed.

At which point, there's a loud boom from down below and the building shakes as a bomb goes off in the basement. Chairs fall over and all around the first floor, things drop off the walls, but nothing much else seems to have happened. Ed Williams instantly grabs Kati Case and hustles her outside, while the rest of the Reps make an orderly withdrawal. The usual large number of tourists is milling around, looking confused. Ed Williams is pushing Kati to get her to a waiting car ASAP, but as she looks at the crowd, she sees a vaguely familiar little bald man with round wire-rimmed glasses looking intently toward the Capitol. Carter Howell's class? And then she has a Holy Shit! moment. The strange student. Guy Fawkes! Wait she yells at Williams, as she grabs the bring-it-everywhere compact camera out of her shoulder pack, zooms in on the little guy, and shoots. He seems to notice and melts into the crowd.

Ed Williams is now all but carrying her to the car. Safely inside, and driving away, he asks "What was that about?"

"I know who did it," she tells him. "This guy." She shows him the photo on the camera screen.

"You know? How?" he asks.

"He was in this class of Carter Howell's at Georgetown. He made this weird comment about Guy Fawkes that didn't make any sense."

"Guy Fawkes? The Halloween mask guy? I don't see -- "

"Guy Fawkes masterminded this plot to blow up Parliament in sixteen-0-something. By putting explosives in the basement. Just like –
"

"Oh. Got it. Give me your camera. Please."

Shortly thereafter, the F.B.I. identifies Maurice Barry, originally of Rangeley, Maine. A couple of disturbing the peace charges years ago. Night janitor at the Capitol. Father, deceased, snow mobile crash. Mother, Québécois, originally from Sherbrooke, whereabouts unknown, possibly back in Canada.

Kati Case's up-to-date photo of the apparent perpetrator is widely circulated by law enforcement and is all over the news, including the amazing fact that the photo was taken by the presidential candidate even as she was being moved to safety. In early afternoon, Maurice Barry is arrested without incident at the Greyhound Station on Massachusetts Avenue near the Capitol, where he has purchased a ticket for Bangor. He has spent the morning desperately and futilely trying to reach Lauren Baxter by phone.

He insists his name is Jesus Leroi and speaks on and off in French. They bring in a translator, but his French is bastardized Quebecois and even she can barely understand half of what he says. Nonetheless, it's clear he readily admits to placing the bomb and setting it off remotely, based on instructions he found on the internet. It was supposed to do more damage. He did it for Lauren Baxter. No, he's not like the guy who shot Reagan to impress Jodi Foster, that was just for sex. Here, he knows that his cher Lauren, although the most beautiful creature there is, also is the one person who knows the extent to which the corrupt government must be brought down. He also admits to firing a shot toward her house, although he can't remember exactly when, when he saw some man who was clearly unworthy of her going out the front door.

By evening, the nation knows, since it's practically the only news story, that because of Kati Case's calm under fire and brave action in the face of danger, a terroristic lunatic has been brought to justice. "It's as if Bush had nabbed Bin Laden right after 9/11," one enthusiastic pundit puts it.

"All I did was take a fucking photo," Kati tells Sheryl Sheldon.

Overnight polling two days later:
VILLAR 46
CASE 45
UNDECIDED 9

Chapter 70

MEMO -- CONFIDENTIAL
10/26

FROM: GENTRY
TO: CASE, DOUGLAS, BLOOM
RE: UPDATE

The Bomber incident has given us significant momentum. National polling is within the margin of error, and essentially shows a deadlock. We are cautiously optimistic that undecideds will continue to break in our direction. However, Villar does maintain stable Republican support, and due to their electoral college advantage, we are at risk of a Democrat again winning the popular vote and losing the election. At the same time, we appear to be competitive in generally Republican states, including North Carolina, Georgia, Ohio and Arizona. If we get the anticipated turnout in Philadelphia from the candidacy of a local, I also have cautious optimism there. Michigan and Wisconsin are up for grabs. As is often the case, it may come down to whether we can turn out more than they can, although unfortunately Republicans tend to be more reliable voters absent some factor that keeps them home. Focus groups suggest that voters are more enthusiastic about Case than Villar as they get to know her. We think it continues to be imperative for her to hit as many places as possible that are competitive between now and Election Day. I would continue to plan on the closing election eve rally at Independence Hall, both because of the optics and to cement the Philadelphia turnout.

Chapter 71

Hey sweet thing,
Turn on the news 11 am Eastern
B

*   *   *

Eleven in the morning is not a convenient time for Kati Case, who is being driven from a morning rally in Toledo to a big lunchtime gathering in downtown Detroit. Sitting in the back of her bullet-proof black Escalade with Mike Bloom, she's trying to get the TruNews app to work on her phone. It's wavering in and out, but she can see what looks like a press conference in front of the Capitol. Unlikely as it seems, Brandon Jarrett is out front. Behind him is a collection of maybe 20 white men, one Latino, and Lydia James, also white, all of whom Kati recognizes as Republican members of the House. Also, an Asian man she isn't familiar with.

"Can you get the volume up?" Bloom asks as she continues to fiddle with the phone.

"I'm here for a reason that's a solemn matter for all of us," Jarrett is saying, drawl turned to the on position. "I don't know if y'all know us, but we're 24 duly-elected Republican members of the House of Representatives. We're here today because we all have reached the unfortunate conclusion that we cannot support our party's candidate for President of the United States."

"Fucking unbelievable," says Bloom.

"He's lost it," says Kati.

"We've reached this decision," Brandon Jarrett goes on, "because we've come to believe that the Republican candidate is not to be trusted. On two pillars of his campaign, his approach to rising sea levels and his proposal that Cuba becomes part of the United States, to put it bluntly, what he's sayin' just ain't true. I'm now goin' to turn this over to two persons who can speak directly to that. First, Professor Park

Dong-wook, a geophysicist from the California Institute of Technology."

"That explains who that guy is," Kati says as the professor, a stocky little guy with neat black hair, approaches the microphone.

"Mind boggling," says Mike Bloom.

"I have studied Mr. Villar's proposal to combat rising sea levels. As I understand it, he would build sea walls and dikes in every vulnerable part of the country. My analysis of this is that except to a very limited extent, it makes no sense." He looks nervous, takes out a white handkerchief and wipes his forehead.

"Why didn't we get a guy like this?" Kati asks. Bloom just shrugs.

"Although in South Florida, sea walls and street elevation has had a slight mitigating effect on the effect of sea level rise, everyone agrees that without serious action to deal with climate change, this can be no more than a very temporary and limited measure. Furthermore, these approaches are completely impractical in most other areas. As to dikes, I can't imagine what he might be thinking, other than that it's the same as a sea wall but he thinks by using a different name it sounds like he's offering an additional solution.

"In short, Mr. Villar's proposal cannot be taken seriously, and it is difficult to imagine that he truthfully believes in it. I don't think this is the time to go into further detail, but anyone who would like to know more should go to noseawalls.com/profpark where my complete scientific analysis is set out. Thank you."

"I'm fucking speechless," Kati says.

Brandon Jarrett is introducing Miguel Machado, Congressman from South Florida. Also, Guillermo Villar's second cousin who, it's commonly known, can't stand him. "This should be really interesting," she adds.

Unlike cousin Guillermo, Machado is tall, thin, clean shaven and passably handsome. "I am truly sorry I have to say what I'm going to say," he starts out, and pauses for effect. "But unfortunately, based on my own personal trip to the island, I have no choice but to tell you that what Mr. Villar has been saying about Cuba is an absolute lie."

"Personal trip?" Bloom comments.

"According to Mr. Villar, some secret source has told him that the Cuban government is enthusiastic about becoming the 51st state. Besides the fact that such unauthorized contact with a foreign government may well be improper, I have discovered first-hand that there's no basis to it."

Kati is desperately trying to take notes in the back of a moving car and simultaneously thinking about where she's fitting this into the speech she's about to give.

"Because of the suspicious nature of Mr. Villar's statements, on the urging and direct authority of President McWillis, I travelled to Cuba just a few days ago and met with several members of the Cuban government. Although no one would speak for attribution, and while the government will continue to refuse any formal comment in the course of our election, I can assure you that there is absolutely no truth to the claim that the Cuban government has any interest whatsoever in becoming an American state, or that anyone in the government there has ever suggested such a thing ."

"Old Clem put him up to this?" says Bloom.

"Guess so," says Kati. "Old foxy grandpa."

Brandon Jarrett is back. "We're all loyal Republicans up here. But sometimes you can go only so far. Now we don't necessarily agree with the Democrats' candidate on a lot of issues. Nonetheless, this is a time when, in particular, we need integrity, stability, intelligence and competence in the White House. So after a lot of serious thought, we've come to the conclusion that we should urge y'all to vote for Kati Case for President. Thank you."

*   *   *

Back in his office, Brandon Jarrett turns his phone on. Nine missed Weatherill calls, six from Beaufort, three from Andrea. He calls Andrea first. "Now I'm one hundred and ten percent positive about you and that Kati Case, that y'all's been fuckin'," she says and hangs up.

As he's considering whether to ignore Beaufort and designate his number as spam, he calls again. Might as well get it over with.

"Boy, you must be out of your mother-fuckin' mind."

"If you say so."

"Don't get smart with me, boy. You're finished. Probably too late to do anything about next week, but then you're dead meat, I'm personally guaranteein' it. And Andrea's havin' the locks changed as we speak, just tell her where to ship all your shit. That prenup's ironclad, my lawyers made sure, so you're gonna need to figure out how to earn a living for once in your life. Have anything to say for yourself, boy?"

"Two things actually. One, I'm not a boy. And two, Beaufort, go fuck yourself."

*   *   *

"Are you out of your fucking mind?"

"Hey, sweet thing, that's about what old bastard Beaufort said."

"You're about the last person I expected -- "

"About the last person *I* expected. But sometimes, you know, you just decide it's time."

"Well thanks. Obviously. How's the wife taking it?"

"She's already changing the locks according to Beaufort."

"B-i-t-c-h. So now what, what're you going to do?"

"I guess I'm employed for two more years. All that's running against me is some retired gym teacher who doesn't have enough money for TV. Even the Weatherill's can't manage a write-in against me in a week. Then, who knows. K street? I'd be good at lobbying, taking all the folks I know out for food and drinks and all. Or maybe just go back to Charlotte and hang a shingle. I'll survive."

Chapter 72

When you're running a "wildly energized campaign" that's "on a mission," according to Lauren Baxter, and you're hitting three cities, sometimes four, every day, it helps to be 37 and Kati Case. The Villar campaign, by contrast, is described as "demoralized," "out of gas," "dead in the water" and other similar cliches the punditry is fond of, and the candidate is managing one rally each evening.

The day before the election, Kati starts in Detroit, barnstorms through Toledo, Columbus and Pittsburgh, and flies on to Philadelphia. Malcolm Douglas is in Atlanta, Charlotte, and Cincinnati before finishing home in Cleveland. Juanita Gomez goes to Tucson, Phoenix and Las Vegas. In Ann Arbor, Sheryl Sheldon and Merrilyn Burnett organize the Michigan College Democrats for the Election Day get-out-the vote effort.

At nine o'clock on a chilly November evening, Kati Case is about to go out to another massive crowd at Independence Hall. This is it, tomorrow there's nothing but voting and waiting. Wally Gentry says the defections of Brandon Jarrett's House Republicans will swing undecideds, independents, and even some Republicans, and cause other Republican voters to just stay home, so he feels good about where they are. Kati hasn't had time to do much reflecting lately, but now, with the end in sight, she suddenly feels a bit overwhelmed. And she thinks of Wilson Burnett, in rehab back in California, and Lenore, who missed it all.

"Thank you, thank you, thank you Philadelphia. Thank you, my hometown. You know," she says, voice rising, "Pennsylvania's had only one President, James Buchanan, and the less we say about him the better. But tomorrow, we're going to change all that." She does her speech one more time, and tells them all to make sure to vote. And then she goes home -- where her father is waiting up for her just like he did when she was out late on a date -- to sleep in what she still thinks, really, is her own bed.

Kati votes early. Ed Williams insists she be driven the two blocks to the polls, rather than walking down 22nd Street like she always has. She goes home and turns on the TV, then turns it off and dozes on the couch while her father reads legal briefs.

Later in the morning, Kati Case and her entourage -- which is with her now wherever she goes -- proceed to the Cardelli Corner Market. The big black cars cause quite a sensation at Sixth and Reed. You can't see out Cardelli's windows for the "Kati Case" signs and banners. Joey Junior greets her and points to a large bowl of "KATI" buttons by the register. "Ain't nobody gettin' served without they're wearing one," he proudly tells her. Grandma Angela gives her a teary hug and yells "Pop, get yourself down, Kati's here." Luckily he has his hearing aids in, he grabs his cane and hobbles down the stairs. Behind the counter, he elbows Joey out of the way. "I'm doing this myself, then I can tell them how I made a Cardelli Special for the next President." Kati's never been a hoagie fan, she hasn't exercised in weeks and she's put on a few pounds, but she gobbles it down.

*　　*　　*

At seven, Malcolm and Glenda Douglas, Mike Bloom and Wally Gentry are sitting together in a suite at the historic Bellevue. Gentry is on the phone with people all over the country. Kati is talking with ward leaders throughout Philadelphia, who report unprecedented turnout. "I want one of those cheesesteaks," Malcolm Douglas says. "OK, but no hot peppers," Glenda tells him, "we learned our lesson."

The cheesesteaks arrive around 7:30, as the polls in Ohio close. Malcolm eats his before he gets on the phone to Cleveland. People are lined up for blocks outside, he reports. At eight, the Pennsylvania polls close, and the lines are even longer.

In the end, it isn't close. Except for South Carolina, every state from Maine to Georgia, plus the District of Columbia, goes for Kati Case. She runs up a 600,000-vote margin in Philadelphia and easily carries Pennsylvania. Sam Jensen manages to deliver New Hampshire and gets himself re-elected. It takes a while, but when North Carolina, and even Georgia, turn blue, it's obvious that Villar's path has become extremely narrow.

She carries Michigan easily, Wisconsin by somewhat less, Illinois and Minnesota by plenty. And then, at around 10, networks start calling Ohio, which has been tight, for Case, and it's all over. Malcolm Douglas vaults out of his seat like he's hauling in a rebound and does a little dance. "Don't go and throw your back out, you old fool," says Glenda, who wipes away a tear. Even before the West Coast, and Arizona, Nevada, Colorado, New Mexico, and Hawaii report -- and she winds up winning all of them -- Kati Case is at 234 electoral votes. California's 55 are never in doubt, and alone they'll be more than enough. Anchoring the TruNews Election Night Coverage, Lauren Baxter makes sure she's the first one to say "President-elect Kati Case."

"Who'd have thought?" Mike Bloom says. "Actually, probably you did."

Kati smiles and squeezes his arm. "Lenore did once say, I was maybe 15, what do you want to do with yourself. I thought it was a stupid question."

"Which you told her, I'm sure."

"Well, I said, I'm 15, how am I supposed to know? Maybe I'll be President. But I wasn't serious. I think."

Guillermo Villar calls. "Now I can say it, I admire you very much. And, you know, if you're looking for some bipartisanship in your administration, give me a call." Heaven save us, Kati thinks, it's starting already.

Juanita Gomez phones in from the noisy ballroom at the San Jose Fairmount.

Her father, waiting at home on Pine Street because he insists it would be inappropriate for the Chief Justice to be at a partisan political gathering -- "for your own daughter?" -- sniffles as he talks to her.

And then she gets a call from Amber Burnett: "Congratulations. He can't talk so well yet, but he insists."

"Kati," Wilson Burnett slowly says, "I couldn't be happier or prouder." He pauses. "What you've done is truly extraordinary, and before long, I hope you'll come to see us and I'll be up and around."

Off the phone, the President-elect excuses herself to the bathroom and has a nice cry.

Mike Bloom says it's time for her and Malcolm Douglas to head down to the ballroom where the crowd and TV cameras await their victory speeches. Kati changes out of her jeans into a black blazer and beige slacks -- what's become the Kati Case signature outfit. They go out to balloons and confetti. They talk about how honored they are, and thank everyone they can remember. They're confident, like everyone else who's made one of these speeches, that they'll be putting the nation on a better course. They hope so.

Installed in his tiny studio on the Near North Side, Lanny Feldbaum finishes a frozen pizza and tries to think of any reason Kati Case might owe him a favor.

In Lakotah Lake, North Dakota, an early season blizzard drops eighteen inches of snow. Randy Carraway comes in from plowing, leaves his boots and parka in the vestibule, and looks at the TV. "Looks like that woman won," his girlfriend tells him. He shrugs. "Any hockey on?" he asks.

Kati waits until she's home to return Brandon Jarrett's call. He's at the Residence Inn, Alexandria. "I needed some privacy," she explains. "I wanted to let you know, I asked my Secret Service guy what happens if the President has, uh, a gentleman caller. He says they're very discreet, it's been a prerequisite for lots of men in the office."

"Well that's more good news. But now, do I still call you sweet thing."

"I hope so," she tells him.

Chapter 73

| CASE | 69,366, 432 | (52.8%) | 339 electoral votes |
| VILLAR | 62,009,387 | (47.2%) | 199 electoral votes |

Chapter 74

    See, Kaitlyn, like I always said, all you need to do is get yourself focused, put your mind to it, and make the effort.
    Thanks, Mom.

Chapter 75

It's snowing lightly outside as Kati Case and her inner circle sit down to an early dinner in the State Dining Room. Kati is making use of her last days not being President by wearing a midnight green Eagles hoodie over a black turtleneck and faded skinny-leg jeans she's pleased she can fit into again after recuperating from months of junk food. A small Christmas tree is set up in the corner. "Kind of formal for my taste in here, I think Old Abe'd thought so too," says Clement McWillis as he points to the grand Lincoln portrait looking down on them. "But this is the part I'm good at, hosting these sit downs, so long as Beryl takes charge of the menu. We've been married 53 years, and I've never missed a meal. Guess I look it."

Mike Bloom, who will be Chief of Staff, is there with his husband. Sheryl Sheldon, who's going to be assisting him in some not quite defined capacity, is there too. "What about Law School?" Kati asks when Sheryl says she wants a White House job. "They'll extend my leave long as I want. It can wait," Sheryl answers. "I once said that," Kati tells her, "and it's still waiting. Well, you worked your ass off. Plus, there was the chicken."

Roger Newley, who's now Kati Case's Press Secretary, is sitting with Marybeth Moran, who shortly will be in charge of all White House cyber operations. "I was happy to just get out of Erie," she says, "who'd have ever thought I'd be on a first name basis with the President, and meet the man of my dreams." She squeezes her fiancés hand. "And she's going to be at my wedding."

"Wouldn't miss it," Kati says.

She and Mike Bloom are already installed in the West Wing, at McWillis's insistence, to accelerate the transition and, he says, "so I don't have to do a damn thing anymore."

Carter Howell, who has been an informal advisor to quite a number of Presidents, has, as always, been consulting with Kati Case. He looks suspiciously at the ribs, grits and collard greens that Beryl McWillis taught the White House chefs to make. The talk turns to what

it takes to be President, after the exhausting travail of running. He pulls a piece of paper out of the inside pocket of his gray tweed jacket and says, "Mario Cuomo, who should have been President but wasn't, once said:
> 'In campaigns, it's all about what you say --
> In government, it's all about what you do --
> And the great ones know the difference.'"

"You just carry that around with you?" Kati asks.

He laughs. "I thought it might come in handy tonight. Because I couldn't be more positive that you're one who knows the difference."

*　　*　　*

Back in her apartment, Kati has a gentleman caller now known to the Secret Service. A Congressman, being divorced by his wife, who's recently switched parties and has been rewarded with the prestigious Chairmanship of the House Ways and Means Committee, a position he's been studying up to prepare for and that will be useful if he subsequently moves into the lobbying field. Next month, when Kati moves out, he also will be renting her apartment on a two-year lease. They talk for a while about what the future may hold, for neither is at all old, and about the futility of planning out relationships. Then they repair to the bedroom, where they get along quite well.

Chapter 76

"Please repeat after me. I, Kaitlyn Cardelli Case do solemnly affirm"

"I, Kaitlyn Cardelli Case do solemnly affirm"

"That I will faithfully execute the office of President of the United States,"

"That I will faithfully execute the office of President of the United States,"

"and will to the best of my Ability, preserve, protect and defend the Constitution of the United States."

"and will to the best of my Ability, preserve protect and defend the Constitution of the United States."

She smiles at her father, who last night attended an Inaugural Ball with Lauren Baxter, and thinks of her mother.

www.ingramcontent.com/pod-product-compliance
Lightning Source LLC
Chambersburg PA
CBHW052047240626
47153CB00006B/2245